THE ULTIMATE SHOWDOWN

A few minutes before one o'clock, Bartlet and his hands started gathering in the street. In another minute, Oates and his boys showed up. They stood facing each other, the dividing line being Slocum's office. Slocum stepped out onto the sidewalk in front of his office and stood watching.

"You men have been itching to have a war with each other for some time, from what I've heard," Slocum said. "Am I right?"

He looked at Oates, who did not answer him. He looked at Bartlet. "Am I right?" Still he got no answer.

"Well, then, get to killing. Here's your chance. We'll find out who the last man standing will be. We'll declare a winner. So pull your guns and start shooting now."

JAKE LOGAN

SLOCUM

IN SHOT CREEK

JOVE BOOKS, NEW YORK

THE BERKLEY PUBLISHING GROUP
Published by the Penguin Group
Penguin Group (USA) Inc.
375 Hudson Street, New York, New York 10014, USA
Penguin Group (Canada), 90 Eglinton Avenue East, Suite 700, Toronto, Ontario M4P 2Y3, Canada
(a division of Pearson Penguin Canada Inc.)
Penguin Books Ltd., 80 Strand, London WC2R 0RL, England
Penguin Group Ireland, 25 St. Stephen's Green, Dublin 2, Ireland (a division of Penguin Books Ltd.)
Penguin Group (Australia), 250 Camberwell Road, Camberwell, Victoria 3124, Australia
(a division of Pearson Australia Group Pty. Ltd.)
Penguin Books India Pvt. Ltd., 11 Community Centre, Panchsheel Park, New Delhi—110 017, India
Penguin Group (NZ), 67 Apollo Drive, Rosedale, North Shore 0745, Auckland, New Zealand
(a division of Pearson New Zealand Ltd.)
Penguin Books (South Africa) (Pty.) Ltd., 24 Sturdee Avenue, Rosebank, Johannesburg 2196,
South Africa

Penguin Books Ltd., Registered Offices: 80 Strand, London WC2R 0RL, England

This is a work of fiction. Names, characters, places, and incidents either are the product of the author's imagination or are used fictitiously, and any resemblance to actual persons, living or dead, business establishments, events, or locales is entirely coincidental.

SLOCUM IN SHOT CREEK

A Jove Book / published by arrangement with the author

PRINTING HISTORY
Jove edition / October 2007

ISBN: 978-0-515-14359-1

JOVE®
Jove Books are published by The Berkley Publishing Group,
a division of Penguin Group (USA) Inc.
375 Hudson Street, New York, New York 10014.
JOVE is a registered trademark of Penguin Group (USA) Inc.
The "J" design is a trademark belonging to Penguin Group (USA) Inc.

PRINTED IN THE UNITED STATES OF AMERICA

10 9 8 7 6 5 4 3 2 1

1

Slocum was damn near broke. He had spent almost all of his cash on booze the night before. He did not even have enough left in his pockets to buy a room for the night, so he had ridden out of town to find a place beside the creek. He had unsaddled his Appaloosa and let it loose, and he had fallen down on the ground and gone to sleep, or passed out, without any other preparation. He knew nothing else until late the next morning. He woke up not knowing what time it was—he knew it was late, though. His head hurt, and he was hungry. He rubbed his eyes and stood up uneasily. He staggered a bit. Then he dug into his pockets for his cash. All he had was pocket change, coins. He counted them and found that he did not have enough for breakfast. He dropped the change back into his jeans pocket and walked down to the edge of the creek.

Stripping off his clothes, he walked into the water for a bath. He knew that he had a sour smell about him from the night before. When he stepped into the water, though, he shivered. It was cold. He forced himself on, getting out to the center and finding the water up to his waist. Taking a deep breath, he bent his knees and got himself in up to his shoulders. He bathed in record time and walked back out of the creek. The sun would dry him off in short order.

He found a clean shirt in his roll. Cleaned up as best as he could get, he headed back for town. Maybe his pocket change would buy him a cup of coffee, a bowl of gravy, and a piece of bread or a biscuit or two. It was a short ride to town, and he stopped at an eatery. He found a table inside and saw a list of dishes and prices on the wall. When the gal came to his table, he ordered biscuits and gravy and a cup of coffee. He had guessed right. It was just all he could afford. She gave him several refills on the coffee, though.

Nursing his last cup of coffee, he heard gunshots outside in the street. He remembered from the night before that this town—what was it called? Oh yeah—this town of Shot Creek was a pretty rowdy place. Slocum thought it should be called Shit Creek. He figured the faster he got out of it the better. The gal waiting tables came back and offered him another refill. He started to refuse it, but then he looked at her for the first time.

She was something to feast a man's eyes on. He was astonished at himself for not noticing her before. He figured her to be about five feet six inches tall and as shapely as she could be. She was wearing jeans and a shirt that showed off her shape to perfection. Her hair was red and long, but she had it tied back to keep it out of her way while she was working. She had big blue eyes and pouty lips. When she refilled his cup, she gave him a smile that warmed his hard heart. He wasn't nearly as anxious to get out of town as he had been before. He was thinking about what he could say to her to strike up a conversation. He was the only customer left in the place.

Just then, though, two men came in. Both were middle-aged, and both were wearing business suits. He glanced up at them just in time to see one give a nod in his direction, and the other one shake his head. Slocum picked up his coffee and took a sip, trying to ignore the two men, but they came walking directly toward him. He noticed that neither man was wearing a gun, at least not where it showed. The men stopped right at the edge of his table, standing directly across from him. He looked up at them.

"You men want something?" he asked.

"My name's Will Church," said the taller of the two men. He took his bowler hat off to reveal a balding head. He sported a handlebar mustache under his nose as if to make up for the lack of hair on top. "This is Mike Fall."

Fall nodded.

"Is your name Slocum?" Church asked.

"It might be," said Slocum. "What's your interest?"

"Can we sit down and talk?"

"Go ahead."

Church and Fall sat down.

"Mr. Slocum," said Church.

"Forget the mister."

"Just Slocum?" said Church.

"That's right."

"All right, Slocum, Mr., uh, Fall here said that he recognized you."

"I get around," said Slocum. "Where have you seen me?"

"I was over at Tombstone," said Fall, "when you, uh, when you killed Three-toed George. I never saw any-thing like it."

"George had it coming," said Slocum.

"I don't doubt it," Fall agreed.

"Three-toed George isn't the only one," said Church. "There have been plenty of others."

"Other what?"

"Other men you've killed."

"What is this?" Slocum asked. "Just who the hell are you men? I mean, besides Church and Fall."

"Oh, I'm sorry, Slocum," said Church. "I'm the mayor of Shot Creek, and Mr. Fall here is on the town council."

"So you dropped by here to say that a notorious gunman ain't welcome in Shit Creek. Is that it? Well, put your minds at ease, gentlemen. I'm leaving right now."

"No, wait a minute, Slocum," Church said. "You got us all wrong. We don't want you to leave town."

"No?"

"No," said Fall. "Far from it."

"Slocum," said Church, "you haven't been in town long, but you've been here long enough to see how it is."

"Fistfights, gunfights," said Fall.

"Sometimes three killings in a day. That's a bad day, but there's an average of three a week for sure."

"No one gets arrested," said Fall.

"We have no lawman," said Church. "This has got to be the worst town in the whole country."

"If it's all that bad," said Slocum, "how come I ain't heard about it?"

"It's off the beaten path. Not many ride through here. We have no railroad, and we have irregular stage service. No newspaper. Some mail shows up and some goes out when the stage comes to town and leaves again."

"What keeps the town alive?"

"There's two big ranches near town," said Church. "A few smaller ones. A lot of cowboys."

"All right," said Slocum, "but what the hell has all this got to do with me?"

"We need a town marshal," Church said.

"Yeah," said Slocum, "I'd say you do."

"We're offering you the job," said Fall.

"I'm no lawman."

"We don't need a lawman," said Fall. "We need a gunfighter."

"I already told you, I'm on my way out of town."

"On your way to what?" said Church.

"The next town, I guess."

"We'll pay you a hundred and fifty dollars a month," said Fall. "Rent you a room in the hotel across the street. Pay for your meals and your drinks."

"And your ammunition," added Church.

"You can hire a deputy of your own choice, and we'll pay his salary," Church added.

Slocum picked up his coffee cup and drained it. The proposition sounded good. It sounded to Slocum like he'd be rich. But he had his pride. A town marshal. A lawman. It damn near made him puke to think about it. He had never stooped so low.

"Well," said Church, "what do you say?"

"I don't think I could stomach the job," Slocum said.

"Not enough pay?" said Church.

"It ain't that."

The gal stepped out of the kitchen just then. "More coffee?" she asked.

"No, thanks," said Slocum. "I'm just leaving."

"I'm sorry," she said. "I didn't mean to be spying on

you, but I heard some of what you were saying. Slocum, I wish you'd reconsider. I wish you'd take the job."

She walked closer as she was speaking, and her big blue eyes were pleading with him. Why the hell did she have to do that? God, she was irresistible. Slocum wanted her in the worst way. He did not want to be a goddamned fucking town marshal. He did not want to stay in Shit Creek. All of his best instincts told him to get out, to run as fast as possible as far away as possible from this town.

"Slocum," said Church, "will you at least think about it? Sleep on it and give us your answer in the morning? We'll pay for a room for you at the hotel and buy your meals till then."

"And I hope we'll continue to do so after that," said Fall.

"You want to start by buying this meal?" said Slocum.

"Of course," said Church.

"Well, I ain't finished eating," Slocum said. He waved a hand at the gal, and she came the rest of the way over to the table. Slocum ordered four eggs, ham, potatoes, more biscuits and gravy. Church told the gal to send the bill to his office. Then he told Slocum where to find him, and he and Fall took their leave.

Slocum ate like it was his last meal, and a part of him thought that it might be—at least, it might be his last meal in Shit Creek. At last he washed it all down with a final cup of coffee. He was the only customer in the place, and the gal came out to join him with her own cup of coffee.

"May I?" she asked him.

"Please do," Slocum said.

She sat directly across the table from him. She smiled,

but he could see through the smile. Underneath it, she was deadly serious. He knew what she wanted; she had already given herself away. She wanted him to stay and take the distasteful job. He wondered if she knew what he wanted. Sure she did, he told himself. A beautiful gal like that. He wasn't the first to lust after her. She had been fighting them off for a few years now. Or not.

"You already know my name," he said.

"Oh, excuse me," she said. "I'm Terri Sue."

"That's a pretty name," said Slocum, "for a pretty gal."

"Thank you," she said.

"But I know what you're up to."

"You do?"

"I do."

"What do you think I'm up to?"

"You came over here to try to convince me to take that job."

"I—"

"It ain't going to be easy, you know. Basically, I have a deep-rooted dislike for all kinds of lawmen. It turns my stomach to think of being one myself."

"Why is that, Slocum?" said Terri Sue.

"Most of them I've met have been bullies and cowards and crooks out to line their own pockets and feel good by pushing folks around."

"Don't you think it would improve things if you were to become a lawman not like the others?"

"It would be one out of hundreds. It wouldn't be much of an improvement."

"But it would be an improvement, however small."

"I never set out to improve the world," he said.

"So what mark will you leave on the world, Slocum?"

"I like to leave things unmarked. Leave them like I found them."

"That's admirable, if things are good when you find them, but if things are bad, it would be more admirable to leave them changed. Don't you think so?"

"I don't know, Terri Sue," said Slocum. "You're getting too philosophical for me now."

"It's not philosophical, Slocum," she said. "It's just plain thinking. That's all."

"I went to war when I was just a boy. After the war, I went home to find my family dead and my home gone. I started wandering, and I've never stopped. I never settled down again."

"You don't have to think of it as settling down. Living in a hotel is not settling down. Just think of it as stopping for a while. You've had jobs, haven't you?"

"Oh, sure. Punching cows. Driving a freight wagon. I've even clerked in a store, believe it or not."

"I believe it. This is no different. It's just a job. Like any other. It can be permanent, or it can be temporary. You can quit and walk away from it at any time."

Slocum looked into her big blue eyes. In his lustful mind, the clothes dropped off her body. He picked up his cup and took a slug of hot coffee to try to drive his thoughts away from lusting after her. He put down the cup and stared at it.

"You sure do have a convincing way of talking to a man," he said.

2

Slocum made his way over to the hotel, where he found that the mayor, true to his word, had reserved him a room. He stashed his stuff in the room and went back downstairs, where he found that he could order himself a bath and send his clothes to a laundry. He did all that, got bold, and ordered a bottle of good whiskey. In short order, he was sitting in a tub of hot water in his room, smoking a cigar, and sipping whiskey from a glass. The idea of being a lawman was growing a little less distasteful to him. A little later, clean, shaved, and dressed in fresh, clean clothes, he walked out onto the street to take a better look at the town.

It was a town much like any other. One street. At the far east end of the street was a livery stable. Across the street from the hotel was the eating place where he had met the lovely Terri Sue. He could see the saloon, which he had become so well acquainted with the night before, and a hardware store, a millinery, a gun shop, a feed store, another saloon, and a general store. He thought about stepping out on the sidewalk like this with a badge on his chest. He shuddered at the thought.

Images of all the lawmen he had ever known floated through his mind. He saw them strut and prance, poking out their bellies, squinting their eyes, turning down the corners of their mouths, their thumbs hooked in the armpits of their vests or in the waistbands of their trousers. He grimaced at the thought and swore that if he ever gave in to the mayor and the councilman and to—well, to the charms of Terri Sue—he would strive with all his might to avoid any of those very noticeable and disgusting lawman habits.

He decided to walk the street to its end, cross it, and walk back down the other side. Really look the town over. It was not crowded at this time of morning, and it seemed peaceable enough. He recalled the gunshots, though, he had heard during his breakfast. He could see a few horses tied in front of each saloon, and he noticed a woman walking out of the general store with a bundle in her arms. A man walked into the gun shop carrying a long-barreled shotgun. Nothing seemed out of order.

When he reached the end of the street, he suddenly realized that he had already started walking with that damned swagger. He was walking like he was really looking things over. He was walking like a lawman. He stopped, took a deep breath, made a conscious effort to put that strut clear out of his mind, and crossed the street. A wagon came racing down the street, and Slocum had to pay attention to it to keep from getting run over. He reached the sidewalk on the other side safely and started strolling back toward where he had started.

He was strutting again. He couldn't figure out how to avoid it. It really pissed him off. He stopped paying attention to the stores and to the people and walked hurriedly back toward the hotel. He was thinking that he should go up to the room, get his things, and get the hell out of this fucking town. It was about to corrupt him. Suddenly his path was blocked. He stopped and looked up to see Mayor Church standing in front of him and smiling.

"Looking our town over, Slocum?" said the mayor.

"Just, uh, taking a walk," Slocum said.

"Well, I'll admit, there isn't all that much to look at, but I think we could have a nice little town here if someone could tame it a bit for us."

"It don't seem too rowdy to me," Slocum said.

"Things are quiet right now," said Church, "but that could change at any minute. It will change almost for sure come evening."

"Mainly rowdy cowhands?" Slocum asked.

"Mainly," said Church.

"What else is there to worry about?"

"Oh, a few ornery kids, occasional domestic squabbles, men that get too drunk and get to spend a night in jail to sober up. You know the kind of things I'm talking about."

"I get the feeling you ain't telling me the whole story," said Slocum.

"You're right, Slocum. Can we talk about it over lunch?"

"Sure."

"About eleven thirty? The same place where you had breakfast this morning?"

Visions of Terri Sue flashed through Slocum's mind.

"I'll see you there," he said.

Just then a man came crashing through a door right across the street. He was moving backward fast, and he fell into the street, landing hard on his back. In an instant, another man came through the door after him.

"You dirty son of a bitch," the man shouted.

He rushed to the fallen man and grabbed him by the shirt, pulling him to his feet. He swung a roundhouse right and smashed it into the man's jaw, knocking him down into the dirt again. The first man was already obviously helpless. The man on his feet walked to the fallen man and kicked him in the ribs. He kicked him again. The man on the ground could only attempt to cover his head with his arms and curl himself into a ball for protection. The third kick was aimed for the man's head. Slocum had taken all he could. He walked out into the street, up behind the man on his feet, the man doing the kicking.

"Hey, pard," he said. "He's had enough."

The man glanced over his shoulder. "Fuck you," he said. He kicked again. Slocum put a hand on the man's shoulder and gripped it hard. He spun the man around and shoved a fist into the man's gut. The man doubled over with a whuff. Slocum grabbed him by the hair of his head and straightened him up.

"I said the man's had enough. Don't you think so?"

"I'll show you what I think, you son of a bitch."

The man drew back his right, but Slocum saw it coming in plenty of time. He blocked it with his left, then hit the man hard on the side of the head with his own right. The man staggered to one side, bent over a little, and shook his head. Then he straightened up, looked hard at Slocum, and suddenly pulled his revolver.

"Slocum, look out," cried Church.

But Slocum had already seen it. His Colt cleared leather and barked before the other's barrel had even gotten level. Slocum's bullet tore into the man's chest, and blood squirted out his back. He staggered back two steps. He tried to raise his revolver, but his arm was weak. His hand lost all its strength. His fingers lost their grip, and the revolver fell to the street. The man's knees buckled and he dropped to a kneeling position. He sat down on his boots and wobbled. Finally he fell forward on his face. He was dead.

Church hurried out to stand beside Slocum in the street. Slocum was helping the fallen man to his feet. Slocum glanced over at Church.

"You got a doc in this town?" he asked.

"Over at the barbershop."

"Can you make it, pard?" Slocum said.

The man was bloody and unsteady on his feet, but he nodded his head.

"Yeah," he said. "I'll make it."

He headed toward the barbershop, and Slocum stood and watched him for a moment.

"So your doc's the barber?" he said.

"That's right. He does a good job."

"At doctoring or barbering?"

"Both," said the mayor. "You handled that situation real well."

"I killed a man," Slocum said.

"It looked to me like he didn't give you any choice."

Slocum looked at the body.

"Well, what do we—"

"I'll take care of that," said Church.

"Well then, I'll see you at eleven thirty."

Church stood and watched Slocum walk away. Then he headed for the eatery. Along the way, he found a man and told him to get Harvey Gool, the undertaker. Then he kept walking. When he reached the eatery, he went inside and found Carl, the owner. He pulled him aside.

"Is Terri Sue working lunch today?" he asked.

"Yeah," said Carl.

"Can you find someone else?"

"What for?"

"Can you?"

"I guess maybe Mabel could do it, but—"

"Then get Mabel," said Church. "I need Terri Sue."

"All right, I'll do it."

Terri Sue came out of the kitchen wearing her apron, and Church took her by the arm and walked to one side with her. She looked at him inquisitively.

"What is it, Mayor?" she asked.

"I just got you a day off," he said.

"What? What day?"

"Today. I'm having lunch here with Slocum, and I want you to join us. Will you do it?"

"Of course I will."

"Good. Eleven thirty then."

"I'll be here."

The mayor turned and left the eatery.

Slocum ducked into the nearest saloon. It was called the Fancy Pants, and it was not the one he had been in the night before. There were maybe half a dozen cowboys in the place. It was quiet. He walked up to the bar and dug into his pockets.

"You're Slocum, ain't you?" said the barkeep.

"That's right."

"Anything you want's on the mayor. My name's Charlie. What'll you have?"

"A glass of whiskey," Slocum said.

Charlie poured him a glass and Slocum took a sip.

"Word gets around this town fast," said Slocum.

Charlie shrugged. "It's a small town."

"You get much trouble in here, Charlie?" Slocum asked.

"Oh, the usual," said Charlie. "A fight ever' now and then. A knifing once or twice a week. A fair number of shootings. Everybody pays for their drinks, though."

"Always look on the bright side," Slocum said.

He sipped his drink slowly and talked with Charlie, but he didn't learn much. He only confirmed that Shot Creek was a rough town, and he already knew that much. Even so, he had a second drink and sipped that one, too, thus extending his conversation with Charlie. He left the Fancy Pants at about eleven twenty and walked to the eatery. He found Mayor Church and Terri Sue sitting at a table inside waiting for him. He took off his hat and hung it over one of the hooks on the wall. Then he walked to their table and sat down.

"This is a pleasant surprise," he said, looking into Terri Sue's blue eyes. She smiled and ducked her head.

A middle-aged woman, pleasant enough, came over to take their order. When she had gone to the kitchen, Church spoke.

"Slocum," he said, "have you given any more thought to my offer?"

"Ain't thought about much of anything else," Slocum said.

"Have you come to a conclusion?"

"It's a tough decision, Mayor," Slocum said.

"The job is a dangerous one," said Church.

"It's not the danger that bothers Slocum," said Terri Sue.

"No?" said Church.

"It's his image."

Church wrinkled his brow and looked from Terri Sue to Slocum and back again. "Image?" he said.

"Slocum thinks that lawmen are a bunch of brutes. He thinks that they're all out for themselves, and they're lawmen because they like to bully people."

Church looked at Slocum. "Is that right?"

"The lady pretty much took the words out of my mouth."

"What you did out there in the street a while ago," said Church, "was just what any good lawman would have done. The only difference is that a lawman would have been wearing a badge and getting a paycheck."

"I just didn't like seeing a helpless man get kicked to death. That's all."

"That's a lawman's job," said Church.

Mabel came out of the kitchen with their meals, so the conversation stopped for a spell. She put the plates of food around and a basket of bread in the middle of the table and refilled all the coffee cups.

"Is there anything else I can do for you?" she said.

"No, thanks, Mabel," said Church. "Everything looks just fine."

"Well, if you need anything, just holler."

Mabel walked back into the kitchen, and the three dug into their meals. The food was good, and Slocum was beginning to feel just a little bit like he was already obligated to Mayor Church and to his town.

3

Slocum did not sleep well that night. He spent some time in the other saloon, the Fat Back, and saw one fist-fight. No one was hurt too bad. Then he went back to his room and settled in for the night, but he did not sleep well. He had visions of himself riding the hell out of Shit Creek, getting away from all the trouble and well away from the prospect of himself wearing a star. It would be a good one on the town, running up a good bill for whiskey, meals, and a room and then running away. It would be the sensible thing to do, and it would agree with his oft-stated philosophy of life: Live and let live. Look out for number one. Mind your own business. Don't stick your nose where it don't belong. There were a hundred ways of saying it, but they all boiled down to the same thing. And sticking to that philosophy was comfortable and usually safe.

But somehow the thought of riding out of Shit Creek having spent all that town money, and having had the lovely big blue eyes of Terri Sue looking hope-fully into his, and having lusted after the sweet Terri Sue—somehow that thought was not comfortable. His philosophy was no longer so simple. Running away would be safer, but it would be disquieting.

And then there were conflicting images running through his brain, images of himself strutting down the sidewalk with his thumbs hooked in the armpits of his vest, his belly sticking out in front of him, a pompous expression on his face, his boot heels clomping on the boards with each step, people scattering in front of him as he walked along. There were visions of himself jerking poor slobbering drunks to their feet and shoving them ahead of him to the jail, where he tossed them in cells, slammed the doors, and locked them, leaving the drunks to moan alone and roll over and puke on the floor of the lonely cell. He saw himself gun down a punk kid, no more than eighteen years old, who was just feeling his oats.

At last he slept, but his sleep was troubled with the same dreams as had been his visions when he was awake. When he got up in the morning, he had not had much sleep. Even so, he dressed and walked down the stairs and out into the street. He crossed over to the eatery and went inside. The place was crowded, but he found a table and sat down. Terri Sue brought him a cup of coffee and took his order. He had three refills before his meal was placed in front of him. By then, several people had finished their meals and left. Mayor Church walked in, spotted Slocum, and joined him at his table.

"Good morning, Slocum," he said. "I hope you slept well."

"Not hardly," Slocum said.

"Something bothering you?"

"I think you know what's on my mind," Slocum said. "It's a big decision for me. Hell, I hate lawmen. If I was to be in a gunfight, I'd rather the other fellow be wearing the badge."

"Then if you won the fight, you'd be on the dodge."

"That's the downside of it for sure," said Slocum. "I know. I've been there."

"I never asked you anything about that," said Church.

"Aw, hell, it's okay. I ain't wanted for nothing just now. Not that I know of."

"Slocum," said Church, "I think I understand your reluctance. I had a few bad run-ins with the law when I was much younger. I've seen the kind of lawmen that you've been talking about. Just because there are so many like that doesn't mean that you'd be like that. You could be the kind of lawman that you think lawmen should be. Clean up a dirty town. Help the good citizens. Do honest work for honest pay."

"You do make it sound good," Slocum said. "Hey, you going to eat?"

"I ate a little earlier," said Church. "Right now I'll shut up and let you eat your meal in peace."

Slocum took a big bite and gave Church a glance. How the hell could he relax with that mayor sitting right across from him? Terri Sue came to refill both men's cups, and Slocum thought that having that filly flitting around was possibly even more distracting. There were two things about her that were bothering him. First, she was in cahoots with Church, trying to convince him to take that horrible job of town marshal. Second, she almost for sure knew what Slocum wanted when he looked at her. He knew that he couldn't hide the lust in his eyes.

He finished his meal and leaned back in his chair to drink his coffee. "Well?" he said.

"Well, what?" said Church. "There's nothing I can say to you that I haven't already said, and there's no point in nagging at you."

"So you got nothing more to say?"

"I'm afraid not. Except that there is something I failed to tell you the first time around."

"Oh, yeah? What's that?"

"I think we may have a range war brewing."

"That's great. Why didn't you tell me about that?"

"It's not in town, so it's not in your—our town marshal's—jurisdiction. I think it *is* part of the cause of all the fights we have in town, though."

"Well, it don't matter now," Slocum said. "I ain't staying anyhow."

"Yes," said Church. "I remember that."

"I ain't seen your pardner since that first time we met," Slocum said.

"You mean Mike Fall? He runs the mercantile just down the street. He's been tied to the store pretty much."

Slocum nodded and sipped his coffee. He drained the cup, put it down, stood up, shoving the chair back, and said to Church, "Well, sir, I thank you for your hospitality. I've thought it over, and I ain't taking the job. I'll be leaving town in a few minutes."

Church stood up and offered his hand. Slocum shook it, feeling a bit guilty.

"Thanks for considering it," Church said. "I won't press. Good travels to you."

Slocum walked out and over to his hotel room. He packed everything up and walked back down to the lobby. The clerk saw him with all his belongings.

"You leaving us?" he asked.

"I'm out of here already," Slocum said.

He stepped out onto the sidewalk and turned toward the livery. He had walked about halfway when a man stepped out of the Fat Back saloon not far ahead of him. The man had the look of a seasoned cowboy. He stood there on the sidewalk, pulled a cigar out of his pocket, struck a match on the wall, and lit the cigar. Across the street, another man skulked in the shadows of the narrow passageway between two buildings. When he saw the cowboy lighting his cigar, the man pulled out a six-gun. Just then, a boy about fourteen years old stepped out of the store next door to the Fat Back and walked in front of the cigar smoker. The man across the street fired. The boy dropped dead in the street. The cowhand ducked back inside the Fat Back. Slocum dropped his gear and jerked out his Colt. The killer turned to run down the passageway.

Slocum ran across the street and between the buildings. The killer was about to disappear around the corner ahead, but Slocum fired a bullet above his head. "Hold it right there," he called out.

The man stopped and stood still for an instant. Then he suddenly whirled and fired at Slocum, the bullet passing just left of Slocum's head. Slocum fired and hit the man in the gut. The killer staggered back a few steps and sat down hard. He held his wound with both hands, and blood flowed out freely between his fingers. Slocum hurried down to the man and kicked the gun away from him. The man wasn't dead, but the way he was hit, Slocum figured it would not be long. Church showed up in the passageway.

"Slocum?" he called out.

Slocum looked back over his shoulder.

"Is he dead?"

"Not yet," Slocum said.

"I'll fetch the doc," said Church.

"Be a waste of time," Slocum said.

The man sitting in the dirt and bleeding in front of Slocum looked up. "You hurt me bad, mister," he said.

"If I'd had a little more time," said Slocum, "I'd have killed you. You killed that boy out there."

"He got in the way," said the killer. "I didn't mean to shoot him."

"I reckon that makes it all right."

"I told you," said the man. "He got in my way."

Slocum felt like putting a finishing bullet into the son of a bitch, but he figured that might get him into some trouble. Besides, maybe it was best to let him die slow. Church came back, bringing the doc and a few other men with him. The doc took a quick look at the wound and told the others to carry the man to the back room of his barbershop. He stood up slowly, looked at Church, and said, "He won't last." The killer groaned when the men picked him up to haul him away. The doc walked off, leaving Slocum and Church alone.

"He didn't give a shit that he killed that boy," Slocum said. " 'He got in my way,' he said."

"That's a typical attitude around here," said Church.

"Why does anyone stay here?"

"Where would we go?"

Slocum ejected the spent cartridge from his Colt and replaced it with a new bullet. He dropped the Colt back into the holster at his side.

"What was the reason for the shooting?" he asked. "Anyone know?"

"I think it had to do with a card game last night," said

the mayor. "Pudge—that's the man you shot—is just a bad loser, I guess."

Then Slocum heard a stifled scream from the street and looked in that direction. Church said, "That'll be Mrs. Bascomb, the boy's mother. I'd better get out there."

He turned to walk back down the passageway to the street. Slocum followed him slowly. He kept his distance as Church put an arm around the woman's shoulder and tried to give her some comfort. Gool, the undertaker, came walking up to the tragic scene. Slocum took a deep breath. He wanted to look away, to look at something else, but he couldn't take his eyes from the boy. He wanted to get back on his way to the livery stable, get his Appaloosa saddled, and ride away from this Shit Creek. He couldn't make himself move.

Terri Sue appeared on the scene. She went to Mrs. Bascomb's side and took her in her arms, relieving the mayor of that burden. Gool ordered some men to pick up the body and carry it to his establishment. Mrs. Bascomb shuddered and wept aloud. As the body was hauled off, Slocum could see Mrs. Bascomb ask something of Terri Sue. Terri Sue answered her and nodded toward Slocum. Then the two women, Terri Sue's arm still around the grieving matron, walked toward Slocum. When they came close, they stopped. Slocum took off his hat.

"I'm sorry for your loss, ma'am," he said.

"I want to thank you for what you done," said Mrs. Bascomb. "It don't bring my boy back, but at least the scum what done the deed won't get away with it. Thank you. Thank you."

Slocum mumbled something, and Terri Sue led the weeping woman away. Slocum ducked his head and shuffled his feet. Then he turned to walk back to where he had dropped his gear on the sidewalk. Mayor Church met him there.

"Just another day in Shot Creek," Church said.

"Shit Creek," said Slocum.

"Well, Slocum, I thank you for one more good deed you did for us. Your last one, I guess."

"You paid for them," Slocum said.

"I guess."

"Did that boy have a daddy?"

"He died a year ago," said Church. "The boy was working for the general store. Trying to help his mother make ends meet. She'll have a tough go at it now—all alone."

"Yeah," said Slocum.

Doc stepped out the front door of the barbershop and looked around. Spotting Slocum and Church, he crossed the street to join them. They both gave him curious looks.

"He's dead now," Doc said. "He died hard, too."

"I wish it could've taken him a little longer to do it," said Slocum. He bent over to pick up his gear.

"Can I walk you to the stable?" said Church.

"No," said Slocum. "You can walk me back to the hotel. I'm staying."

"You're staying? You mean—"

"I mean I'll take the goddamn job. It's still open, ain't it?"

"Not now," said Church. "You just filled it."

They walked to the hotel together. Slocum tossed his gear on the counter. Church said, "Dobe, will you take this stuff back to Slocum's room? He's staying on with us. Permanent."

"For a time," said Slocum.

"For a time," Church corrected. "Slocum, let's go look at your office."

4

Slocum could not bring himself to sit behind the big desk in the marshal's office. He paced the floor for a bit and then took one of the chairs that lined the wall to his right. Mayor Church walked around behind the big desk and opened a drawer. He reached in and withdrew a badge. It was a big star, and across its front the words TOWN MARSHAL were imprinted. Taking the star, Church walked around the desk and over to where Slocum was sitting. He held the star out toward Slocum. Slocum stared at it, scarcely believing what he was doing. He did not move. Church leaned forward and pinned the badge to Slocum's shirt. Then he straightened up again and stepped back.

"All right?" he said.

Slocum did not answer. He was stunned. He sat, staring down at the offensive badge on his chest.

"It looks good there," said Church.

Slocum heaved a heavy sigh. "If you say so, Mayor," he answered. "Well, hell, I said it and I'll stick to my word. We'll at least get this town calmed down some before I move along."

"I'm sure we will," said Church. "Thank you again. Now, I think everything in here is obvious. Gun rack over there with ammunition drawer. Check it over and see if it has everything you need. If it doesn't, just get what you want at any store in town and charge it to the mayor's office."

"Yeah," Slocum said. "Well, I'll be all right. Oh, yeah. You got a printer in this town?"

"Tony Dawson, just down the street here a few doors."

"A good carpenter?"

"Orvel Davis. He's working down at the stable right now. I can go see him and—"

"I'll find him," Slocum said.

The mayor went back to his office, and Slocum walked down the street to the printer. He left instructions on what he wanted and told Dawson to bill the mayor's office. Then he walked toward the stable. He was self-conscious walking the sidewalks in daylight with the star on his chest. It gleamed in the sunlight. It felt heavy. He felt like everyone on the street was looking at him. No. Looking at the badge. He was relieved when he reached the stable and went inside.

"Can I help you, mister? Oh, it's you. You want your horse saddled?"

"No, old-timer. I ain't going nowhere. I'm looking for Orvel Davis."

The livery man was staring at the badge.

"You the new marshal, are you?" he asked.

"I reckon you can see," said Slocum. "Davis?"

"Uh, he's out back." The man gestured to the back door, which was totally unnecessary. The doors were big and obvious and in the back wall. Slocum headed for them. One of the big doors was already ajar, and he stepped through it. A man was out there measuring a board. He looked up as Slocum stepped out.

"Orvel Davis?" said Slocum.

"That's me."

"I'm Slocum."

"The new marshal."

"I got a job for you."

"What is it?" Davis asked.

"I want you to go over to the Fancy Pants and build a rack behind the bar close to the front door designed to hold guns. Lots of guns. All kinds. Then I want you to go to the Fat Back and do the same thing there. Send your bill to the mayor's office."

"It'll likely be tomorrow morning—"

"Now," said Slocum. "This job can wait. Mine can't."

He turned and walked back through the stable and out into the street. He had half the length of the town to go to make it to his office. Once again, he felt the heavy weight of the star and the stares of all the people along the street. A couple of people spoke to him as they passed him by. A few others just nodded. At last he made it to the office. He went inside and just stood in the middle of the floor. He had never felt so uncomfortable before in his life that he could remember. He walked over to the gun cabinet and opened the drawer. Inside were several boxes of cartridges for both his Colt and his Winchester. There were some other kinds of guns in the cabinet, and there was ammunition for them, as well. Slocum did not care about them.

He had a dilemma. He did not think he could stand being in the marshal's office. He wanted to get out, but he could hardly take the people outside looking at him with the badge on his chest. He thought about taking the star off and dropping it down in his shirt pocket. But most everyone had already seen him with it, so it really shouldn't matter if he went out again with it still showing. If he took it off, there would be questions. He decided that he would go on out. He wanted some more coffee.

He walked back to the eatery and went inside. It was the middle of the morning, and no one was there. He picked out a table and sat down, and in another minute, Terri Sue appeared.

"Well, hello," she said.

"Coffee," said Slocum.

Terri Sue brought him some. "Can you stand some company?" she asked.

"Sit down," he said. "How's the Bascomb woman doing?"

"Not very well," Terri Sue said. "Mr. Gool will be burying her boy this afternoon."

"I guess I'll go and pay my respects," Slocum said.

"That will be nice. She'll appreciate that. I know she will."

"Well, it won't do her no good, but I reckon it won't hurt anything, either."

"You're wrong about that, Slocum," Terri Sue said. "It will do her some good. Slocum?"

"Yeah?"

"What have you been doing all your life?"

"After the war? Drifting around. Getting in and out of trouble."

"That's all?"

"What else is there?"

"Settling down. Making a decent living."

"Getting a wife and having a bunch of kids?"

"Well, that, too."

"No woman ever owned me, Terri Sue. Never will, neither."

"I guess I can see that. You need some more coffee?"

"No, thanks. That one will do me. I got something to take care of. Thanks for the coffee, and the company."

"Any time, Marshal."

Slocum winced at that.

"Just put the coffee on—"

"On the mayor's bill," she said. "I know."

Slocum walked out and made his way back to Tony Dawson's print shop. Dawson was ready for him. Slocum took the posters he'd had printed up and walked to the Fat Back saloon. Orvel Davis was inside, already working on the gun rack. Slocum got a nail and a hammer from Davis and tacked up a poster beside the gun rack. It said: CHECK GUNS HERE. ORDER OF THE MARSHAL. Then he went back outside and tacked the next poster just outside the saloon's front door. This one read: ALL GUNS MUST BE CHECKED INSIDE. ORDER OF THE MAR-SHAL. He walked down the street to the Fancy Pants and did the same thing there. He went back to the Fat Back to return the hammer. As he turned to go back outside, a cowboy stood in his way.

"You think you can get away with that in Shot Creek?" he said.

Slocum jerked a thumb toward the poster. "You mean that?" he said.

"Hell yes. You know what I mean."

Slocum looked down at the six-gun hanging at the man's side.

"You'll be the first," he said. "Unbuckle your belt."

"I don't ever do that," the cowhand said.

"I bet you do," said Slocum. "I bet you take it off to go to sleep at night. To fuck. To take a shit. All you have to do is just add one more thing to that list. To go in a saloon and take a drink. I ain't going to wait much longer."

"Take it away from me," the cowboy said.

He reached for his gun, but Slocum was much faster. Before the puncher could clear leather, Slocum had whipped out his Colt, raised it high, and brought the barrel down hard on the man's head. The man's eyes glazed. He seemed frozen in position for an instant. Then he fell forward onto the floor. Slocum leaned forward and rolled the man over onto his back. He unbuckled the man's gunbelt and pulled it loose from his body. Then, throwing the belt over his shoulder, he took hold of the man's collar and started dragging him toward the jail.

On the sidewalk, a young man stepped up. He was dressed like a cowboy and had a friendly, smiling face.

"Can I help you?" he said.

Slocum said, "Grab hold."

Together they dragged the unconscious body to the marshal's office and inside to a cell. Slocum shut the cell door and locked it. He tossed the keys onto the big desktop. Then he turned to look at the young man. "I'm Slocum," he said, holding out his hand.

The young man took it to shake, and said, "My name's Tommy Howard," he said. "I'm glad you took the mayor's offer. Billy Bascomb was a good friend of mine. Oh, it's true I'm a few years older than he was, but he was a good kid. I'm going to miss him."

"I just wish I could have stopped it."

"The way I heard it, there wasn't no way you could've done nothing but what you did. Say, I want to ask you something."

"Well, go on."

"You need a deputy?"

Slocum looked at Tommy. Looked him up and down. Tommy was wearing a gun.

"Can you use that thing?" Slocum asked.

"I can handle it all right," Tommy said. "I can hit a target. I ain't never shot a man."

"Can you do paperwork?"

"I can read and write, and I can do figures."

"If you'd been my deputy a while ago, I'd have just had you haul this silly bastard down here by yourself."

"That's all right."

"How old are you?"

"Twenty-one."

"I reckon that's all right." Slocum walked to the desk and opened the door he recalled Church opening to fetch his badge. Sure enough, there were others in there. He picked one up and looked at it. It read: DEPUTY MAR-SHAL. Slocum walked to Tommy and handed him the badge. "Pin this son of a bitch on," he said. "Then walk over to the mayor's office and tell him I've hired you."

Tommy grinned a wide grin and pinned on the badge. Still smiling, he looked up at Slocum. He took Slocum's hand and pumped it. "Thank you, Mr. Slocum," he said. "Thank you."

Slocum pulled his hand loose. "You might not be thanking me before long," he said. "And you can forget that 'mister' bullshit. I'm just Slocum. Get along now and see ole Church."

"Yes, sir, mister, uh, Slocum. Yes, sir. I'll be right back."

He turned and nearly ran out the door. Slocum watched him go. He had mixed feelings about this young man. He could be getting the boy killed. He hoped not. Hell, he had been younger than that boy when he'd gone to war, and he had survived it all right. He'd learned to take care of himself along the way, too. If Tommy could keep from getting himself killed, Slocum thought, he might just learn something.

Slocum left the office just as the cowboy in the cell was coming to and groaning. He headed for the eatery. It would be noon real soon. Along the way, he saw Tommy come running out of the mayor's office. Tommy saw him, too, and ran to meet him.

"Slocum," Tommy said, "he put me on the payroll."

"He'd better," said Slocum. "I hired you."

"Yes, sir."

"I was just headed for some lunch. You want to join me?"

"Yes, sir. I'd sure admire to."

"And cut out that 'sir' stuff. You ain't in the damn army."

"Yes—Uh, yeah. Okay."

It was a little before noon, and there were already a few customers in the place. Terri Sue was at their table right away, though. She looked at the badge on Tommy's shirt.

"New deputy, huh?"

"That's right," said Slocum. "This is—"

"I know Tommy," she said. "Congratulations, Tommy."

"Thanks, Terri Sue."

He was still smiling. Just then, Mike Fall came in. He was followed by Will Church. Soon Slocum's table was full, and Slocum felt crowded. The main thing on his mind was Terri Sue.

5

Toward evening, when the saloons started to fill up, Slocum and Tommy walked into the Fat Back. There was a pretty good-sized crowd in there already, and most of them were packing guns. Slocum was wearing his Colt. He had given Tommy a loaded shotgun to carry along. Slocum walked to about the center of the bar, where there was a space, and backed up against it so that he was facing most of the crowd. There were a few men to his right and to his left standing at the bar. Tommy backed up to the bar beside Slocum. There was too much noise in the Fat Back to get anyone's attention any other way, so Slocum pulled out his Colt and fired a shot into the air. The place got quiet, and all eyes turned his way. The stars on his and Tommy's chests were very visible. Slocum looked around the room.

"In case you ain't figured it out," he said in a loud and clear voice, "I'm the new town marshal. Name's Slocum. Tommy Howard here is my deputy. Now, I'm going to assume that some of you can't read, and the ones that can read just didn't notice the new signs. There's one outside the door and another one right over there beside the new

cabinet. The signs say that you have to check your guns
when you come into the saloon. I can see ain't none of
you done that, so you can start doing it right now."

No one got up. No one made a move to comply.

"If you ain't going to cooperate," Slocum said, "I'll
just have to start taking them from you."

A big cowhand sitting at a table near the bar laughed
out loud, and everyone else joined in the laughter.
Slocum walked over to the big man's table. Before anyone knew what was going on, he jerked out his Colt and
bashed the man over the head. Out cold, the man's head
dropped to the table and hit it with a thud. Slocum took
the gun out of the holster and handed it to Tommy, who
put it on the bar. The nervous barkeep took it and put it
in the cabinet.

Slocum turned to another man. This time, the man
gave up his weapon easily. Slocum went around the room
collecting guns. Soon the new gun cabinet was stacked
up with guns. Slocum moved toward the last table in the
place, and a snotty little brat wearing two guns stood up
snarling.

"I don't give up my guns to no man," he said.

"You're awful young to die for such a silly reason,"
Slocum said.

"Who said I'm going to die?"

"You will if you don't give me those guns," Slocum
said. "Or if you don't want to give them up, you can
leave. Right now."

"I ain't going to do neither," said the kid.

"It's your call," Slocum said.

The crowded saloon was as quiet as the wee hours
of morning when everything was closed and locked up
tight as a Klondike miner's butthole. The kid stepped

out a couple of paces from the table, keeping his narrow, mean eyes on Slocum all the while. He flexed the fingers on both hands.

"Kid," said Slocum, "you don't have to do this."

"You're the one come looking for trouble, Marshal."

"All I want is your gun. You can have it back when you leave."

"No way," said the kid. Both of his hands streaked for the six-guns at his sides. They had just cleared leather as Slocum's Colt roared and his bullet smashed the sternum of the kid. The young gunman's face registered total surprise. His eyes opened wide. His mouth hung open. His fingers went limp, and both his guns dropped to the floor. He staggered back a few steps and backed into the next table. The men sitting there grabbed hold of it to keep it steady. The kid's knees buckled, and he dropped to the floor on them. His eyes glazed over, and he pitched forward—dead.

Slocum looked around. "Anyone else got anything to check in?" he said. The remaining three men with guns then unbuckled their belts and laid them on the table. Tommy picked them up.

"You men have a good time," Slocum said. "Let's go, Tommy."

They walked out of the Fat Back and down the sidewalk till they came to the Fancy Pants. Inside, Slocum noticed right away that the gun cabinet in there had a few guns in it. At least some men were cooperating. He walked up to the bar, followed by Tommy, and Charlie, the barkeep, came over to greet them.

"Any guns out there?" Slocum asked.

"A few," said Charlie. He pointed out a couple of tables. Slocum looked at Tommy.

"You take that one over there," he said. "I'll take this one."

The two lawmen headed for their respective tables. Slocum reached his first.

"You boys see the new signs?" he said.

The three men at the table all looked up at him. They looked sheepish. One man finally answered. "Uh, yeah," he said. "We seen them."

"You ain't checked your guns," Slocum said.

"I guess we didn't take it serious," the man said.

"Yeah," said another. "We thought it was a joke."

"It's no joke," Slocum said. "I'll take your guns now."

The men all shucked their weapons, and Slocum picked them up and carried them to Charlie at the bar. Charlie took them and toted them to the cabinet.

At the other table, Tommy had asked the same questions. There were four men at the table, and they were engaged in a game of poker. The tabletop was covered with cards and money. Two of the players shoved their chairs back. One man stood up. The man standing was the first to speak.

"Sonny boy," he said, "I don't think you're man enough to take our guns."

Tommy blasted the tabletop with his shotgun, scattering cards and money. Two of the players dropped to the floor and covered their heads. One man squealed. Some of the shot had glanced off the tabletop and peppered his face. Most of it had dug into the table. The wounded man's hands went up to his face. The man who was standing went for his six-gun, but Tommy swung the scattergun around to cover him. He stopped.

"There's another shot in this here gun," Tommy said.

Slocum looked over at Tommy, unbelieving. He walked over to the table quickly.

"We'll take those guns now," he said.

The men all took off their weapons and laid them on the table. Slocum gathered them up.

"You can all pick up your guns when you leave," he said. "We don't expect any more trouble here tonight."

They left the saloon and walked to the marshal's office. Inside, Slocum sat down in the chair behind the big desk. Tommy replaced the shell in the shotgun. Then he put the shotgun in the gun rack. As he turned away from the rack, he saw that Slocum was staring at him.

"Something wrong?" he asked.

"What the hell made you do that?" Slocum said.

"What?"

"What? What the hell do you think? What made you shoot that scattergun back there?"

Tommy shrugged. "It seemed like the thing to do," he said. "It damn sure got their attention, didn't it? The fellow who thought he wanted to shoot it out changed his mind."

"I got to admit that."

"Look," said Tommy, "I knew that at that close range, the shot wouldn't scatter out much. I didn't hurt no one. Not much anyway. That one shot did exactly what I figured it would do."

"It sure as hell fucked up that poker game," Slocum said.

Both men laughed at that. Then Slocum told Tommy to keep an eye on things. He announced his intention of going to bed and getting some sleep, but he told Tommy his room number at the hotel and said, "If you need me for anything, come and get me."

He left the office and walked to the hotel and upstairs to his room. He found the door unlocked, looked a little puzzled, then opened the door and stepped inside. The small lamp on the table was lit and turned down low. Terri Sue was sitting in the chair and smiling at him. He shut the door and locked it. Taking off his hat, he tossed it onto another chair.

"This is a surprise," he said.

"A pleasant one?" asked Terri Sue.

"That depends on what you're doing here."

"Well, I'm not sure. It depends a lot on you."

Slocum unbuckled his gunbelt and hung it over the back of a chair. He walked toward Terri Sue, and she stood up to meet him. He put a hand on each of her shoulders and leaned forward to kiss her on the lips. She responded delightfully. Slocum stepped back to pull off his shirt. In another moment, they were both naked. Slocum picked Terri Sue up and carried her to the bed. He placed her easily on the mattress, and then he crawled in beside her. They rolled toward one another to kiss once again. Slocum's right hand found her left breast and clutched it. He massaged it, delighting in the softness and the smoothness of it. She moaned through their kisses, enjoying the feel of his hand on her breast.

Slocum was thinking ahead, though. He was impatient. His tool was standing out by this time, long and hard and throbbing. His hand moved from her breast down her body to the hairy tuft at her crotch. It was damp. He prodded for the slit and felt between the lips with his finger. It was wet and slippery. He dug deeper until his finger slid into the hole.

"Umm," she groaned.

She rolled over onto her back, pulling him on top of

her as she did and spreading her legs to allow him to lie between them. As he crawled into position, Terri Sue reached down low with both her hands and found his rod.

"Oh," she said. "I think you're ready to go."

"More than ready," he said.

She aimed the tip of his tool for her slit and rubbed it up and down, getting it nice and wet and slick. Then she put it into her hole, and Slocum drove it forward.

"Ahh. Oh," she gasped.

As he thrust his cock all the way into her tunnel of love, she wrapped her legs around him and crossed her feet on his back. She thrust her loins up to meet his downward thrust.

"Take that, baby," he said.

"Oh. I'll take it and more. Oh. Oh."

Slocum drove in and pulled out over and over again. She responded to each of his thrusts with one of her own. They went faster and faster, harder and harder until at last, the pressure built up inside Slocum's loins was too much to contain, and he shot forth, burst after burst, deep inside her.

In the Fat Back saloon a fistfight started. No one saw it begin. It was just going on. Two cowhands pounding on each other. They knocked over several tables and broke a couple of chairs. The crowd gathered in the saloon yelled and cheered them on, each rooting for his personal favorite. Most of the crowd was on their feet, screaming and hollering. At last one man knocked the other through the swinging batwing front doors and out into the street. He ran through the doors after his intended victim. The other man was just getting up and met him with a roundhouse right, knocking him back through the doors and into the crowd that had rushed up to the door to watch the action in the street.

The crowd caught the man and shoved him back outside. Some of them followed him out. Others stayed at the doors, watching. As the man went back out, he was met again with a right that staggered him. This time he turned his back on his rival and pushed his way back through the crowd into the Fat Back. He made his way to the gun rack and grabbed a six-gun. Cocking the gun as he went, he pushed his way back through the crowd. The man outside stood in the street waiting, but when he saw the other come through the crowd again, gun in hand, his eyes widened.

"Hey," he shouted. "I ain't armed."

"You're dead, you son of a bitch," the armed man said, and he pulled the trigger. A bullet smashed into the man's chest. He staggered backward and fell.

"You've killed him," someone shouted.

"He asked for it," said the killer.

In the marshal's office, Tommy Howard heard the shot. Jumping up, he grabbed the shotgun from the rack and hurried outside. He could see the crowd on the sidewalk in front of the Fat Back, and a moment later, he could see the body in the street. He ran toward the scene. As he got closer, he could see the man with the gun standing facing the crowd as if threatening them. He ran up closer and stopped, the shotgun pointed at the man with the six-gun in hand.

"Hold it right there," he said.

The man turned, noticing Tommy for the first time. His six-gun was aimed vaguely in Tommy's direction.

"Even if you hit me," Tommy said, "this scattergun will tear you to pieces."

The man dropped the gun, and Tommy gestured with the shotgun toward the jail. The man started walking. In the hotel room upstairs, Slocum had thrown open the window. Tommy noticed it as he passed by. He looked up and grinned.

"Everything's under control, Marshal," he shouted.

6

Slocum had breakfast in the morning, and then he started checking up on the events of the night before. There were plenty of witnesses to the murder; there was no doubt that Tommy Howard had the right man in jail. He went to see Will Church. The mayor had already heard the tale.

"So what do we do now?" Slocum asked.

"We'll have a trial, of course," said Church. "We're so out of the way here that we've had to learn to do things for ourselves. The council decided some time ago that the mayor would be the judge. That's me. I see no reason to prolong things. We'll set the trial for Monday."

"That's just four days from now," said Slocum.

"That's plenty of time. I've heard that Hyde already has a lawyer."

"Hyde?"

"Sammy Hyde. That's the man you have in jail. He works for the Simple Simon Ranch. Simon Oates owns the place, and he has his own lawyer. There can't be much of a defense anyway. He shot down Bennie Dill in

47

front of plenty of witnesses, and Bennie didn't even have a gun on him."

"What's my role in this?" Slocum said.

"Keep Hyde in jail till Monday, and then make sure that he's in the courtroom on time. Make it ten o'clock in the morning."

"He'll be there," said Slocum, and he left the office.

Later that morning, Slocum saw Tommy in the marshal's office.

"Hyde's trial is set for Monday morning at ten," he said. "You did a good job last night, Tommy."

"Thanks, Marshal," said Tommy.

"You put the coffee on?"

"Yes, sir."

Just then six men rode up in front of the office. They dismounted, and two of them walked to the door. The older of the two opened the door and walked in, followed by the second man. The older was a tough-looking fellow with a sandy-brown handlebar mustache. He had a slight middle-age paunch to his belly, and he was wearing a Colt at his side. His companion was dressed similarly but was smooth-shaven and younger.

"What can I do for you?" Slocum said.

"You can let my man out of jail," said the older of the two men.

"Your man?" said Slocum. "You mean Hyde?"

"Who else you got in there?"

"He's being held on a murder charge," said Tommy.

"His trial's set for Monday. He'll stay in jail till then, and after that, likely he'll hang," Slocum said.

"I'll put up his bail."

"Bail ain't been set. Probably won't be on a murder charge."

"Marshal," said the younger man, "maybe we come in here too hasty. We should've made some introductions. I'm Mo Diamond. I'm the foreman at the Simple Simon Ranch, and this here is my boss. This is Mr. Simon Oates."

"I'm the new marshal. Slocum's the name. And this here is my deputy, Tommy Howard. There still ain't no bail."

"We'll see about that," said Oates. He walked over to the cell, where Hyde was standing, clutching at the bars of the door and looking anxious.

"Boss," he said. "Get me out of here."

"You goddamned fool, Sammy," said Oates. "Why'd you do it?"

"I was drunk, Mr. Oates," Hyde said. "Ole Dill, he was mouthing off about you and the ranch. We got into a fistfight. Our guns was checked in. We fought our way outside and back in and then out again, I think. Well, he punched me up pretty good, and I run back inside and got my gun, and I-I shot him. That's all."

"You're a fucking blockhead," said Oates, "but don't worry. You won't hang. I'll see to that."

"I wouldn't make no bold promises like that," said Slocum.

Oates turned and gave Slocum a hard look. "I don't make promises," he said. "I just state what it is I mean to do. Come on, Mo."

"Be seeing you, Sammy," said Diamond, and he followed Oates out the door.

Tommy Howard walked to the window and watched

as the Simple Simon crew rode over to the office of the mayor. "They went right straight to Church," he said.

"That figures," said Slocum.

"Mr. Oates will be right back to get me out of here," said Hyde. "He'll likely have you both fired, too. You'll see. Nobody around here bucks Mr. Simon Oates. Nobody."

Slocum walked to the stove and poured himself a cup of coffee. "Shut up, Hyde," he said.

"All right, but I'll have me a cup of that there coffee."

"You ain't in jail to be waited on," Slocum said.

"They're leaving the mayor's office," said Tommy. "Looks like they're riding out of town."

"What?" said Hyde.

"You heard me right," said Tommy. "They're leaving town."

"Damn it. There's going to be hell to pay for this."

"I told you to shut up," said Slocum.

Tommy walked over to Slocum's desk and sat on the edge, looking hard at Slocum. "He's right, you know," he said. "Oates is used to getting things his way. He ain't going home to sit quiet."

"What do you think he'll do?"

"My bet is that he'll try to bust Sam out of here before Monday."

"How many hands has he got at the Simple Simon?"

"Oh, I ain't sure. Around twenty, I'd say."

"The odds ain't good," Slocum said.

Hyde laughed out loud from inside the cell. "If you're smart," he said, "you'll unlock this cell right now and let me out."

A bucket of water stood near the far wall. Slocum stood up and walked to it. He picked it up and strode to the cell. Then he pitched the bucketful through the cell door onto Hyde. Hyde sputtered and fumed.

"I'm smart enough to keep my mouth shut when I've been told to," Slocum said. He dropped the empty bucket on the floor and walked to the front door. "I'm going to see the mayor," he said. "Hold down the fort."

Slocum crossed the street to Church's office and went inside. He found the mayor just putting on his hat. When Church saw Slocum walk in, he put the hat back on the hat rack. "I was just coming to see you," he said.

"You just had a visit from Simon Oates," Slocum said. "He wanted you to set bail for Hyde. Right?"

"That's right," said Church, going back to his desk. "He didn't take it kindly when he didn't get his way."

"So you turned him down."

"Of course I did. We have a town marshal now. With a deputy. If we mean to make this stick, we have to have law and order. I'll back up your office all the way."

"I don't know how much good that's going to do if Oates rides in here with twenty men," Slocum said.

Church looked thoughtful for a moment. "And he's apt to do just that," he said. "I'll see how many men I can raise here in town."

"That would be an idea," Slocum said.

The door opened and a man dressed like a rancher stepped into the office. "Howdy, Will," he said. "I assume that this is your new marshal, Slocum."

"It is, Bill," Church said. "Slocum, this is Bill Bartlet. He's the other big rancher around here."

Slocum and Bartlet shook hands. Bartlet said, "I understand you've got that Sam Hyde in jail."

"That's right," Slocum said.

"Bennie Dill was one of my boys," said Bartlet. "I

came in because I heard that Simon Oates was in here to see you."

"He was here all right," said Church. "He stopped in the marshal's office first, and then he came to see me."

"I guess he didn't get what he wanted from the marshal then," said Bartlet. "Did he have any better luck here?"

"He rode away angry," said Church.

"That's what I want to hear," Bartlet said. "I just want to make sure that Hyde hangs for what he did."

"I can't promise you that," Church said. "All I can promise is that he'll get a fair trial. I can tell you, though, that there were plenty of witnesses, and they all said that Dill was unarmed."

"I have an idea," said Slocum. "Someone said that Oates might come in here with his whole damn crew to take Hyde out of jail."

"I can have my whole crew in town to see that he don't," said Bartlet.

"You took the thought right out of my head," Slocum said. "What size crew you got?"

"I have twenty-four cowhands," said Bartlet.

"Mayor," said Slocum, "when you warned me that there might be a range war looming, you weren't talking about these two, were you?"

Church looked sheepishly at Bartlet. "Well, yes, I was."

"Bartlet," Slocum said, "if there's a chance of something like that brewing, I wouldn't bring my whole crew into town. Half maybe. Me and Tommy will make it fourteen. That ought to be enough. I doubt if Oates will bring in all of his at once, either."

"It'll be a war right here in town," Church said.

"Maybe not," Slocum said. "It might just be a stand-off."

"Oates won't dare try anything if he sees me and my boys in town," said Bartlet. "I'll get back out there right now and come back with a crew."

Bartlet rode out of town, leaving Slocum and Church alone in the office.

"The range war might come sooner than I thought," said Church.

"Yeah," said Slocum. "It might. And we'll be fighting with one crew. I hope it don't look like we chose sides."

"We'll just be upholding the law," Church said. "Oates has threatened to stop the trial. We have a right to deputize citizens. If those citizens happen to work for Bill Bartlet, that's just the way it is."

"Well, I think I'd best go inform my deputy of what we've schemed up over here."

"You mind if I go along?"

"Nope. Not a bit."

They walked together across the street to the marshal's office, where Tommy sat alone except for the prisoner sulking in the cell, his clothes still sopping wet. Church noticed him dripping in the cell.

"What happened to him?" the mayor said.

"Oh, nothing much," said Slocum. "He was just talking too much is all."

Church looked from the prisoner to the empty water bucket on the floor and then at Slocum. He looked back at Hyde. "If I were in your shoes," he said, "I believe I'd keep my mouth shut."

Hyde grumbled but said nothing.

"Tommy," said Slocum, "let's go have a drink."

"Right now?"

"That's right. Come on."

"What have I done?"

"Nothing. Me and the mayor have done something."

As they went out the door, Slocum looked back at Hyde and said, "Don't go anyplace till we get back." They walked to the Fancy Pants. The first thing they noticed was that none of the customers was wearing a gun.

"Get us a table," Slocum said. He stopped at the bar and got a bottle and three glasses from Charlie. Then he joined Tommy and Church at an out-of-the-way table, where they could talk without being overheard. Slocum poured the glasses full. They each took a drink.

"Tommy," said Slocum, "remember what you said about Oates riding in here with twenty men to break Hyde out of jail?"

"Sure. I remember. He just might do it."

"That's what we told Bill Bartlet."

"Bartlet?"

"Yeah," said Church. "He came to see me in my office. Slocum was there at the time."

"It seems that the man Hyde killed was one of Bartlet's crew," Slocum said. "Bartlet wants to see Hyde hang. Bartlet said he'd send in half his crew to keep Oates from breaking Hyde out."

"Well," said Tommy, "it sounds like it might keep Hyde in jail till the trial all right, but it might just start—"

"Start the range war," said Slocum.

"It's a chance we have to take," the mayor said. "This has been brewing for a long time now."

7

The town filled up amazingly quickly. Simon Oates showed up first with twelve men. They rode directly up to the jail. They did not dismount. Oates shouted out in a bold voice, "Slocum. You in there?" The door opened and Slocum stepped out onto the sidewalk. He did not speak. He just stood, staring straight into the eyes of Oates. "I want Sam Hyde, Slocum," Oates continued, "and I mean to have him."

"You mean to go against the law?" Slocum asked.

"We've got along here just fine without no law," Oates said. "You going to unlock that cell, or do I have to turn my boys loose?"

Slocum looked around at the "boys." He noticed that Mo Diamond was conspicuously absent. It looked to Slocum as if Old Man Oates had brought in about half of his crew. He figured that Diamond had been left behind at the ranch to manage things out there. Maybe also because he seemed to have a cool head. Oates needed hotheads for this job.

"Just say the word, boss," said a cocky young kid sitting horseback next to Oates.

"Well, Slocum?" said Oates.

The door to the office opened again, and Tommy Howard stepped out to stand beside Slocum. He was carrying the shotgun.

"It'll take more than two of you to handle us," said Oates.

"This here scattergun will handle you, old man," Tommy said. He lifted the barrel and pointed it directly at Oates. "If I see anyone even look like he's going for a gun or thinking about dismounting, I'll pull this trigger. And at this range, it'll blow you in half."

"It might take a couple of men close to you as well," said Slocum.

"Boss?" said the smart-ass kid next to Oates.

"Shut up, Breezy," Oates said.

"We going to stand around looking at each other all day like this?" Tommy asked.

At just that crucial moment, another group of riders appeared. Oates turned in the saddle to see what was going on just as Bill Bartlet rode up with ten of his men along. They stopped, their horses facing Oates on his left.

"Bartlet," said Oates. "What the hell are you doing here?"

"We heard there's going to be a trial," Bartlet said. "We came early to make sure nothing goes wrong. What are you doing?"

"Just came to town for a drink," said Oates. "Come on, boys. Let's get on over to the Fancy Pants."

"Don't forget to check your guns when you go in," said Slocum.

Oates turned his horse and led the way to the Fancy Pants. Bartlet rode up closer to the jail. "It looks like we got here just in time," he said.

"I'd say so," said Slocum.

"Aw, hell," said Tommy, "we had everything under control."

"Since you've got such control," Slocum said, "why don't you take that shotgun down to the Fancy Pants and make sure all those men check their guns."

"Why, shore, daddy," said Tommy, and he headed for the Fancy Pants saloon with a wide grin on his face. Slocum looked up at Bartlet. He nodded toward the Fancy Pants.

"He's left a man on the street to watch the jail," he said.

"I'll leave a few out to watch him," Bartlet said.

"Let's put a couple of them in the jail," Slocum said.

Bartlet selected two men to go inside the jail, and two more to stay out on the street. He and Slocum and the rest of his hands headed for the Fat Back. Along the way, they met Tommy.

"All disarmed in the Fancy Pants," he said.

"Bartlet left two men at the jail," Slocum said. "Why don't you go back there and hang with them for a spell?"

"Sure thing," Tommy said. He headed for the office, while Slocum and Bartlet and the cowboys continued on their way to the Fat Back.

In the Fancy Pants, Oates sat at a table with the slick kid he'd called Breezy and a couple of other cowhands. The rest of his men were scattered around the room, some sitting at tables, a few standing at the bar. Breezy downed a whiskey, and it went to his head right away.

"Boss," he said, "how come we're sitting around in this damn saloon without our guns? What the hell are we going to do?"

"I've got to think of something, kid," Oates said. "If that Bartlet bunch had come in just a little later, we'd have Hyde out of there. Now, it looks like it'll be a big fight."

"Me and the rest of the boys ain't afraid of a fight," said Breezy.

"Are you suggesting that I am?"

"Well, you—"

"Listen to me, smarty pants," Oates said. "I ain't afraid of Bartlet and his bunch or of the law. I just don't want to turn this town into a battleground if it can be helped, and I don't want to get any of my crew killed unnecessarily. I mean to get Hyde out of jail, like I said. I look after my boys. But I mean to do it without bloodshed if I can."

"They ain't going to turn him loose without a fight, boss."

"I know that. Just be patient, Breezy. Our time will come."

"Bartlet means for that trial to go on," Breezy said. "He wants to see Sammy hang."

"I know that, Breezy. And you know my intentions."

Breezy reached for the bottle and poured himself another drink. He knew his boss's intentions, all right, but he did not go along with his methods. Patience was not one of Breezy's few virtues. He was a two-gun kid, and he was fast with both hands. It was his way to dive right into a situation and get things done. He downed the drink fast and reached for the bottle again. Oates grabbed his wrist.

"Breezy," he said, "I think you've had enough."

One of Breezy's few virtues was loyalty and obedience to his boss. He did not argue. "Yeah. Okay, boss," he said. "I think I'll go out for some fresh air." He stood up, a bit wobbly on his feet, and he felt a little light-headed. He did his best to stand and walk straight. He went out onto the sidewalk and stood for a moment, looking around and trying to regain control of his legs. He saw the Bartlet men on the sidewalk. He took deep breaths. He started walking.

He walked down the street till he came to one of Bartlet's men. He nodded, tipped his hat and smirked, and walked on by. In another minute, he found himself at the jail. He paused, then walked boldly inside. The two Bartlet men stood up quickly, hands on the butts of their six-guns. Tommy swung the barrel of the shotgun up and ready.

"Hold it right there," he said.

The kid smiled and raised his hands.

"I ain't looking for trouble," he said. "I just want to talk to Sammy there."

"I guess there ain't no harm in that," Tommy said. "Take off your gunbelt."

The kid unbuckled his belt and held it out toward one of the cowhands, who took it and then sat back down. Breezy walked on over to the cell. Sam Hyde was at the door, clutching the bars.

"When am I getting out of here?" he said.

"I ain't sure about that, Sammy. The boss is over in the saloon with the boys. He's got about a dozen of us in town, but then old Bartlet has got a bunch of his boys in town, too. It's a kind of a standoff, I guess."

"If we have that trial on Monday, they're going to hang me," said Hyde.

"Well, now, we don't mean to let that happen."

"What're you going to do?"

"I ain't sure. The boss—"

"When?"

"I don't know, Sam. The boss don't want to start a war in town."

"I don't give a damn about that," said Hyde. "It's my neck I'm thinking about."

"Yeah. I know. Be a little more patient with us, will you? Something might happen real soon."

Breezy turned away from the cell and walked to the door. He looked at the cowhand who was holding his guns.

"I'm leaving now," he said. "Can I have my guns back?"

The cowhand glanced at Tommy, and Tommy nodded. The cowhand held out the gunbelt, and Breezy took it and strapped it on. Then he stepped outside. He stood for a moment thinking, a task he was not much good at. Then he walked to the Fat Back and went inside. All the Bartlet hands looked at him, as did Slocum. Breezy stepped up to the bar and ordered a shot. Slocum got up and moved to the bar beside Breezy.

"You forgot to check your gun," he said.

"Oh, yeah. Sorry, Marshal," Breezy said. He downed his whiskey in a gulp. "I'm just leaving. I think I come into the wrong place anyhow."

He walked back outside feeling big and bold. He decided that he could get Sammy Hyde out of jail without any help. He was fast with his guns. He thought that he could step in the door of the marshal's office and gun down all three men before they even expected it. He was that fast. He did not know of any fast guns working for Bartlet, and as for the deputy, well, he was just Tommy Howard. Tommy had been around town for quite a spell. No one had ever paid any attention to him. He had no reputation. Since he had become Slocum's deputy, he had pulled off a couple of deals by bluff, by waving that shotgun. He was nothing. He pulled out his Colts one at a time and checked them. Then he slid them in and out of the holsters. He was ready.

He walked back to the marshal's office and jail and went around back to try the door. He found it locked. So he would have to use the front door. He walked around to the front and opened the door, stepping in quickly and jerking out his Colts. The two Bartlet cowhands jumped up and jerked at their Colts. Breezy fired two quick shots, dropping both cowboys. Tommy fired the shotgun, blasting Breezy back through the door and into the street.

Slocum heard the shots and rushed out of the Fat Back. He saw the body in the street as soon as he stepped outside. He ran the rest of the way to his office. Even with the chest and face all messed up from the shotgun blast, he could see that the corpse had been Breezy. He stepped into the office. Tommy was standing there looking at the two dead cowboys.

"What happened here?" he asked.

"That fool kid just stepped in and started blasting. He killed these two before I could shoot. I got him then, though."

"I can see that," said Slocum. He stepped back outside. Some men were already gathering on the sidewalk. Slocum turned to one of them and said, "Go get Harvey

Gool." The man turned to run down the street. Slocum walked to the Fancy Pants and found Oates still sitting at his table.

"Your gunman is dead," he said.

Oates looked up at Slocum. "What are you talking about?" he asked.

"You don't know? You didn't hear the shots?"

"I heard the shots. What were they?"

"Your kid gunslinger walked into my office and started shooting. He killed two Bartlet cowhands before my deputy got him."

"So Breezy's dead. I told him to be patient."

"You didn't send him over to break Hyde loose?"

"No, Marshal, I did not. I did not want anyone to get killed over this business."

"I think everyone would be better off if you took your crew back out to your ranch," Slocum said.

"I don't think you have the authority to order me out of town," Oates said. "I haven't broken any laws."

"One of your men did."

"And he's dead."

"Well, you've been warned," said Slocum. He went outside and walked to the Fat Back, where he told Bartlet what had transpired. Bartlet left the saloon to go to Gool's establishment and look at the bodies. He paid Gool for two caskets and burials. Then he went back to the Fat Back and told his hands they would have a funeral that afternoon. He assigned two more men to stay at the jail with Tommy. Then he had another glass of whiskey. Slocum reached for the bottle and also poured himself another. He looked at Bartlet.

"You know it's started," he said.

"I know."

"You've lost three men now, and Oates has lost one."

"It won't stop here," said Bartlet. "It won't stop now. Not until one of us has lost. Clearly and definitely. Till one of us is dead or has left the country."

8

It was early the next morning, following a particularly tense night during which nothing of note happened, when a stranger rode into town. From the front window of the marshal's office, Slocum noticed him in particular. He had the look of a gunfighter, but there was something else about him. There was something familiar about his features. He rode easy. He was somewhere in his thirties. His face was clean-shaven, and he was dressed like a cowboy going to town on a Saturday night—wearing polished black boots with his tight, black trousers tucked into them. He had on a white shirt with a thin black tie, a black vest, and a flat-brimmed black hat. Blond hair showed underneath it. Around his waist was buckled a black leather gunbelt with a black holster on each side. His guns were Colts. He stopped in front of the Fancy Pants saloon, dismounted, and tied his horse. Then he walked inside.

Slocum stepped over to the stove and poured himself a cup of coffee. He was in the office with two Bartlet cowhands. Tommy was somewhere asleep. He had been on duty most of the night. Sammy Hyde was lying on his cot in the cell. Slocum set his coffee down on the desk, took out a cigar, and lit it. Then he picked up the coffee and walked to the cell.

"You must be one hell of a cowhand," he said.

Hyde lifted up his head and looked through the bars at Slocum. "You talking to me?" he said.

"Ain't no one else in there," said Slocum.

"Well, I ain't so bad, but what made you say that?"

"Your boss is willing to start a range war to keep you from hanging," Slocum said. "It could cost a bunch of lives."

"Ain't nothing I can do about it," said Hyde. "'Course, you could."

"You mean just turn you loose?"

"Why not?"

"Because we got law in this town," Slocum said, "and there's going to be a trial."

"Not if Mr. Oates has anything to say about it," said Hyde.

"He means to talk loud," Slocum said. "It looks like he's just hired himself a new gunfighter."

"Oh, yeah?"

"I think I'll walk over and give him a Shit Creek welcome." Slocum turned away from the cell. He put his cup down on the desk and turned to the two Bartlet hands. "Boys," he said, "don't open this door to anyone except me or Tommy. Hyde gets no visitors."

In the Fancy Pants saloon, the stranger had spotted Oates right away and walked straight to his table. He had then introduced himself and been invited to sit down. Oates had advised the man about the rule regarding guns in the saloons. The man had taken off his guns and handed them over to Charlie, the barkeep. Then he sat down. When Slocum walked in, it looked like the two men were old friends. Slocum went to their table.

"Sorry, there ain't no room to invite you to sit down, Marshal," Oates said.

"You hire yourself a new gunfighter, Oates?" Slocum said.

"This here's a cowhand," said Oates. He looked at the stranger, and the stranger nodded. "Yeah. He's working for me."

"What's your name, stranger?" Slocum said.

"Richard Cherry," the stranger said. "What's yours, Marshal?"

"Slocum."

"Slocum?" said Cherry. "I've heard of you, but I sure never expected to find you behind a badge."

Slocum felt his face flush. "I reckon I ought to apologize for that," he said. "Anyhow it's a long story. Right now I'm more interested in what brought you to town."

"I got nothing to hide," Cherry said. "A while back I got a letter from a cousin of mine. He said he thought there might be some trouble brewing up this way. He suggested I come by and look for a job. He was working for Mr. Oates here."

"You say he *was* working?"

"He's dead now," said Cherry.

"His name was Breezy," said Oates.

"I see," Slocum said.

"Don't worry, Marshal Slocum," said Cherry. "I won't be going after your deputy. I heard how it happened. Breezy was hotheaded. There wasn't nothing else the deputy could have done."

"I'm glad to hear you say that," Slocum said.

Cherry shoved his chair back and stood up. "Mr. Oates says there ain't no room at the table," he said. "Will you step over to the bar and let me buy you a drink?"

"Sure," Slocum said.

Oates gave Cherry a disgusted look but kept his mouth shut. Cherry walked Slocum to the bar and Charlie brought two glasses and a bottle. Cherry paid and then poured the drinks.

"Just between you and me, Slocum," he said, "I never knew Breezy all that well. I heard through the family that he admired me and was jealous of my reputation. He was trying to imitate me."

Slocum then realized the familiar look Cherry'd had to him when he first saw the gunfighter ride into town.

"Yeah," he said. "I could see that."

"He was doing a pretty good job, huh?"

"He looked all right, but like you said, he was hot-headed."

"Yeah. Slocum?" Cherry reached out and touched the badge. "How'd this happen?"

"The mayor tried to hire me, but I told him that I hate lawmen. Then I saw a kid shot down in the street. I talked to his mother. There was no law here. None. I decided to take the job and see if I could kind of straighten this town out. When I get that done—"

"If you get that done," Cherry interrupted.

"If I get that done, I'll turn in this goddamned badge and get the hell out of here."

Cherry smiled and shook his head, looking down at the bar. "Slocum," he said, "you got a real soft spot."

"Don't count on it," Slocum said.

"You taking sides in this range war?"

"I'm taking the side of the law," Slocum said, a little

ashamed of what he was saying. "One of Oates's cowboys shot an unarmed man. I've got him in jail waiting for trial. Oates came into town with a dozen cowboys to get him out of jail. That's when I asked Bartlet for a little help. So Bartlet's boys are like deputies. Does that explain it?"

"So this is all over one possible hanging?"

"There's been bad blood between Oates and Bartlet for some time from what I hear, but this one deal has set it off."

Cherry looked thoughtful and poured two more drinks. "Tell you what, Slocum," he said. "I won't interfere with the trial or with the hanging, if it comes to that. You got my word."

Slocum nodded. "All right," he said. "I appreciate that."

"When the hanging's over and done," Cherry said, "this deputy deal with the Bartlet hands is over with, too. Right?"

"That's right."

"Well then, you and me can be friends, can't we?"

"Let's wait till the job is over," Slocum said. "Then we'll see."

When Slocum returned to the office, he found Tommy sitting behind his big desk with the shotgun on the desktop in front of him. Two Bartlet cowhands were sitting in chairs, smoking cigarettes. Hyde had been talking, but he shut up when Slocum entered the room. Perhaps he was recalling the sudden bath he had taken once before for talking too much.

"Everything quiet?" Slocum asked.

"Yeah," said one of the cowhands.

"So far," said Tommy.

"Tommy, let's take a walk."

"Okay."

Tommy reached for the shotgun. "You can leave that," Slocum said. Tommy shrugged and followed Slocum out of the office. Slocum led the way across the street. The sidewalk was less crowded over there. They walked along for a few steps in silence.

"Did you see that stranger ride into town this morning?" Slocum asked.

"That two-gun man? Yeah, I seen him."

"He's a professional gunfighter. Name's Richard Cherry."

"Have you heard of him before this?"

"I've heard of him," Slocum said. "I went over and had a talk with him just now. That fellow whose head you blowed off was his cousin."

"Yeah?"

"That's right. But he says he didn't know him all that well, and the cousin was hotheaded. He knows that you didn't have no choice. He ain't after you."

"Well, that's some relief."

"He's working for Oates, but he told me he won't interfere with the trial or the hanging. After that, all bets are off."

"That's an interesting twist," said Tommy.

"Yeah," said Slocum. "Listen to me now. One reason I'm telling you all this is to warn you to keep your eyes open. I tend to believe that Cherry, but don't count on it. He might be a good actor. Watch him. I mean to."

Slocum sent Tommy back to the office and walked over to the eatery to get a bite and some good coffee. He also wanted to see Terri Sue again. He found three tables occupied and Terri Sue more or less free. Everyone had their meals. Terri Sue brought Slocum some coffee. Then she sat down.

"Slocum," she said, "is there going to be trouble in town?"

"That's hard to say," Slocum answered. "Oates brought his boys to town to break Hyde out of jail, but Bartlet brought his in to keep Hyde in jail. Right now, it's kind of a standoff. Oates just brought in a new gunfighter, who told me that he means to stay out of it till the trial's over."

"Do you believe him?"

"I'm trying to."

"Hey, gal, bring us some more coffee over here," one of the customers called out.

"Be a little patient there, pard," said Slocum. "We're talking official business. She'll be with you in a minute."

"Official business, my ass," said the man. "I know all about you two. Bring me some more coffee, damn it."

Slocum stood up and walked to the man's table. "You've got a dirty mind, mister," he said. "I don't think you need any more coffee. Just pay up and get out."

Terri Sue rushed to the table with the coffeepot.

"It's all right, Slocum," she said. "Here's the coffee."

Slocum put a hand on her shoulder and gently but firmly pushed her aside.

"I think you heard me," he said.

The man stood up. He was bigger than Slocum, and from his looks, he had weathered more than his share of fights.

"That badge don't mean nothing to me," he said. "If I was you, I'd let the gal refill my cup."

"You ain't me, and I ain't you," Slocum said. "I told you to pay up and clear out."

The man looked down and away and then suddenly swung a roundhouse right at Slocum's jaw. Slocum saw it coming but just barely in time. He dodged and caught a glancing blow along the side of his head. Slocum raised his right foot and brought the boot heel down hard on the big man's left foot, cracking a few small bones. The man howled and raised his foot and grabbed it with both hands. Slocum stepped quickly behind him, took hold of his shirt collar, and walked him to the door, shoving him through it. The man sprawled in the street, still holding his foot and moaning. Slocum shut the door and went back inside. Terri Sue was refilling all the coffee cups in the room.

"That's okay," said the man whose cup she was refilling. He was looking at Slocum, who was moving back toward his own table. "That's plenty," he added nervously. "Thanks."

Terri Sue returned to Slocum's table.

"I could've handled that," she said.

"Well, I did handle it. Put his meal on my bill with the town."

"That was Pete James, Slocum," she said. "He's mean and tough, and he doesn't forget or forgive."

"He's a bully and a blowhard," Slocum said. "He doesn't scare me."

Outside, Pete James sat seething, still holding his foot with the broken bones. He decided to go get his gun, which was inside his saddlebag. He started to get up, but when he put weight on his foot, the pain was just too intense He cried out and settled back down. The foot was starting to swell; he could feel it. He knew he had to get the boot off. He took it in both hands and tried to pull, but that, too, hurt excruciatingly. He lay over in the dirt so he could reach into his trouser pocket. He came out with a knife, which he unfolded, and then proceeded to cut the boot off his foot.

The door to the eatery opened, and Slocum came walking out. He looked at the man sitting in the dirt. Pete James snarled and flung the cut boot at Slocum, but it missed him by several feet.

"Forget it, pard," Slocum said. "I paid for your meal."

"I ain't forgetting nothing, mister," Pete James snarled. "You dirty son of a bitch. I'll kill you."

9

"You mean to do that today," Slocum said, "or do I have to wait for your foot to feel better?"

"Right now I can't even stand up on my feet. A fight now just wouldn't be fair."

"You mean to have a fair fight with me?" Slocum said. "A fair gunfight?"

"That's what I'm meaning."

"Well, mister, you'd better be handier with guns than you are with your fists, or you'll be a dead man. You want me to help you up on your horse?"

"I don't want nothing to do with you till I kill you."

Just then, another man came walking along the sidewalk. He paused and looked at Pete James sitting in the dirt. Then he looked at Slocum. Slocum did not appear to be a threat, so he walked on over to the man sitting in the dirt wearing one boot.

"Pete?" he said. "You need some help?"

"Yeah," said James. "Help me to my feet and over to my horse, would you?"

"Sure thing."

The man reached down and helped Pete James up to

75

his one foot. Every time the injured foot touched the ground, Pete squealed. He put an arm around the other man's shoulders and hopped on his good foot over to his horse. When he got there, he leaned with both arms on the saddle and panted awhile.

"You want some help up?" said the other man.

"No," said Pete. "I can swing up in the saddle okay by myself. Thanks. You can run on now."

"All right. If you're sure about it."

"I'm sure. Run on now."

The other man walked back to the sidewalk and headed on down the street. Pete waited a moment, then slipped his Henry rifle out of the saddlebag. He could see Slocum walking away toward the jail. He cranked a shell into the chamber of the Henry and laid the rifle across the saddle. He took careful aim at Slocum's back, right between the shoulder blades. He licked his lips and started to squeeze the trigger, but he lost his balance a little just then, and his injured foot automatically went to the ground to steady him. When it touched the dirt, he flinched and squealed, and Slocum turned to see him there with the rifle.

Pete James recovered quickly and aimed the rifle again, but Slocum's Colt was out of the holster and blazing away before Pete could fire. Slocum's bullet tore into Pete's forehead. Pete dropped the rifle on the opposite side of the horse from where he stood as he started to slide to the ground. Slocum could see his hands on the saddle. Then they disappeared, and Slocum looked underneath the horse's body to see the man's body crumple up once again in the dirt. Pete James did not move. He would never move again.

"I seen it, Marshal," a man on the street said. "He was trying to back-shoot you."

"Yeah," said Slocum. "Thanks. You think you could fetch ole Gool down here to clean up this mess?"

"Be glad to, Marshal."

Slocum winced at being addressed that way. He wanted to get this job over with and get the hell out of town and hope that the word would not spread. He did not want this job added to his reputation.

"Oh, uh, Marshal?" the other man said.

"Yeah. What is it?"

"I reckon you know who that man is—the one you just killed?"

"I got no idea."

"His name was Pete James. He worked for Mr. Oates."

"That figures," Slocum said. "Well, go on now and fetch Gool."

"Yes, sir, I will."

Slocum walked down to the Fancy Pants saloon and stepped inside. Oates and some of his boys were sitting around a table drinking whiskey. Richard Cherry was with them. Slocum walked right up to their table and looked at Oates. Oates looked back at him.

"What is it, Slocum?" Oates said.

"I want to be the first to tell you," Slocum said. "I just shot your man Pete James."

"Dead?"

"Dead."

"How come?"

"He asked for it," said Slocum. "He tried to back-shoot me with a Henry rifle. There were witnesses."

"I don't doubt your word," said Oates. "Where's the body?"

"I sent for Gool to take care of it."

Slocum shot a glance at Cherry, but Cherry just gave a shrug. "It's nothing to me," he said. "I didn't even know the man."

"Slocum," said Oates, "sit down and let me buy you a drink."

That was the last thing that Slocum expected. He decided to stick around and see what the old man was up to. The chairs at the table were all occupied, so Slocum reached for one at the next table, intending to pull it over. Oates said to one of his men, "Get up and give him your chair." The man picked up his glass and moved out of the way, and Slocum sat down. Oates called out for another glass, and when it was brought to the table, poured it about half full of whiskey. Slocum looked at it and looked at Oates.

"Drink up," Oates said.

Slocum picked up the glass and took a sip. Oates drank some of his.

"Slocum," he said, "there's something you need to know."

"I'm all ears."

"Pete James was always looking for trouble. I wouldn't even be upset except that I always look after my boys. It's a matter of principle. If they're loyal to me, I look after them."

"Sort of like you're looking after Sammy Hyde?"

"Just like that."

"That's admirable up to a point, but Sammy Hyde's a murderer, just like James would have been if I'd been a little slower."

"I can't help that," said Oates.

"You're willing to start a range war on behalf of Hyde, but you mean to let my killing of James just go by?"

"Sammy's still alive," Oates said. "That's the difference."

Slocum took another sip of whiskey. "I don't think we're getting anywhere with this conversation," he said.

"Well, I didn't stop you to philosophize with you," Oates said.

"What then?" said Slocum.

"Pete James had some pretty good friends among my boys. I'll tell them to let it go by, but I can't guarantee their behavior."

"It's real big of you to warn me," Slocum said.

"I want to avoid any unnecessary trouble."

"Then take your 'boys' back out to your ranch and let this trial go on the way it's supposed to."

"I would, Slocum. I would, but I can't let Sammy hang."

Slocum downed the rest of his drink and put the glass back on the table. Then he stood up.

"Thanks for the drink," he said, and he turned and walked out of the saloon. He walked to the hotel and went up to his room. He wanted to be alone to have the peace to think. He wanted to think about the mess he had gotten himself into. It was a pretty bad deal wearing a badge. He was ashamed of himself. But he had taken a job, and he had never before taken a job and not seen it through. He was stuck. He had to finish the job. He tried telling himself that it couldn't be all that bad. All he had to do was stick with it until the trial was over and done with and Hyde was hanged. Somehow he had to make sure that a range war was not started over Hyde's fate. If the men started a range war, then the job would become more complicated. He would have to hang around until the range war was ended and the community was peaceable.

When the hanging was over with and the range war was either prevented or concluded, he would have to stay until he was sure he had cleaned up the town. But that was it. That would be the end of the job. At that point, he could get the hell out and hope that he would be leaving the horrible incident behind him.

Then he thought of Terri Sue. She was just fine, but even she was not worth what he was doing to his self-respect. Maybe he would give her another tumble or two. Maybe not. She did help to pass the wretched time in this wretched place. Of course, when the romp was over with, he still had the mess to deal with.

There was Sammy Hyde, guilty as sin, no question about it, sitting in jail waiting for his trial on Monday, just around the corner. There was his boss, Oates, and his large crew, hanging around town, having meant to break Hyde out of jail but having been prevented from doing so when Bartlet and his crew, all friends of the murdered man, had come to town to aid the marshal in keeping Hyde in jail until the trial.

Chances were that a large-scale range war would develop out of this mess. Even if Hyde were to make it to trial, it was almost certain that Oates and his crew would resort to violence to prevent the hanging. In the meantime, there was Slocum, embarrassingly the town marshal, sitting in the middle of these two factions that were nearly at war with one another. There he was—

But he did have a deputy, and he had the help of the Bartlet ranch hands. So Tommy Howard and two of the ranch hands were watching over Hyde in the jailhouse. Why the hell had Slocum not thought more about that? That meant that he could stay in his room. Or he could stay in a saloon and drink. Hell, he could stay drunk. Tommy could handle everything with his shotgun and the voluntary help of the Bartlet ranch hands. Slocum decided that he would get drunk.

He got up and walked downstairs and outside and then over to the Fat Back saloon. Bartlet and some of his men were sitting around drinking whiskey. Slocum nodded at them, but he walked straight to the bar and ordered a bottle and a glass. Instead of opening the bottle, he took it by the neck and took up the glass and walked back outside.

"Slocum," Bartlet called out.

"Whatever it is," Slocum said over his shoulder, "see Tommy about it."

"But—"

"He can handle it."

Slocum kept walking. He went back to the hotel and upstairs to his room. He shut the door, put down the bottle and glass, hung his hat on a peg, took off his gunbelt and slung it across the back of a chair, sat down on the edge of the bed and pulled off his boots, pulled his shirt off, popped the cork off the bottle, and poured a glass full of whiskey. Then he flung himself onto the bed and started sipping the whiskey.

For the first two glasses, his thoughts did not change much from where they had been. After two more glasses, he had a new idea. He drank some more, thinking about this new idea. The more he thought about it, the more he liked it. It made good sense. It would solve everything. Well, perhaps it would not solve everything, but it would certainly ease the situation for a while. Or maybe it really would solve everything.

He could not predict what kind of response he would get from either Bartlet or Oates, but any way they responded to his proposal would be an improvement over how the situation stood currently. By God, he would do it. He would put the plan into action. He would—

He started to get up off the bed but did not make it. He fell back again onto the pillow. He tried again, using all his energy, making a supreme effort. He moved more slowly and carefully and managed to get up to a sitting position. His head was swimming. He had to go out into the street and set off the plan, so he stood up, but his legs were wobbly. He stood there for a moment.

At last he could stand upright, so he made a step toward the chair where his gunbelt was hanging. He reached out for the gunbelt. He lost his balance and fell over flat on his back on the floor.

"Shit. Goddamn it," he said.

He rolled over onto his stomach and managed to get up to his hands and knees. He reached up and put a hand on the back of the chair, but instead of pulling himself up, he pulled the chair over. He just did not have the strength to try again. He rolled over onto his back again. He decided that he would stay there and sleep it off. He hoped that no one would start anything until he was better the next morning. The next morning should be time enough to set the plan into motion. He hoped that when he had sobered up, he would still remember it.

10

"Hey, Deputy," said Sammy Hyde.

Tommy was sitting behind the desk, fondling the shotgun he had grown so fond of. "What do you want, Hyde?" he said.

"I want a drink of whiskey. You got some in your desk. I know it."

"We don't serve drinks to prisoners," Tommy said.

"Come on," said Sammy. "What'll it hurt? Huh?"

"What do you think, boys?" Tommy said to the two Bartlet hands who were sitting in the office with him.

One of them shrugged. The other one said, "I don't think it would matter a damn if he was to get drunk. In another couple of days, he's going to hang."

"Well, all right," Tommy said. He put the shotgun down on the desktop and opened a desk drawer, taking out a bottle and a glass. He stood up and poured the glass full, then carried it to the cell.

Sammy Hyde reached through the bars for it. He drank about half of it in one gulp. "That's more like it," he said. Tommy turned to go back to the desk, but Hyde stopped him. "Tommy," he said, "wait a minute."

Tommy turned back to the cell. "What is it now?" he said.

"I want to talk to you."

"Well?"

"Come here. Come closer."

"Don't you try anything."

"What? With those two Bartlet hands in here? I just don't want them to hear what I have to say."

Tommy stepped up close to the bars. "Well, go on then," he said.

"Why don't you turn me loose?"

"Why don't you shut up?" Tommy said, starting to leave.

Sammy grabbed his arm through the bars. "Wait. Listen. Keeping me in here will just start a big fight. Everyone knows that. If you let me out of here, I'll ride away from these parts. The range war won't happen. At least, not account of me, it won't."

"That makes good sense," said Tommy. "There's only one problem with it."

"What? What problem?"

"I'd lose my job, and I like my job. Tell you what I'll do, though."

"What'll you do?"

"I'll pour you another drink."

"Aw, come on, Tommy."

"You get drunk enough, you won't give a damn about getting out of here."

"Oates and them will kill you when they finally bust me out of here."

"They might try."

Tommy walked back to the desk for the bottle, but

just as he stepped behind it, the front door opened and two Oates hands appeared. "We want to see—"

Tommy grabbed the shotgun and blasted twice. The two men flew back into the street.

"Goddamn," said one of the Bartlet hands.

Tommy reloaded the shotgun quickly. Both Bartlet men had jerked their six-guns out and run into the street. Tommy snapped the gun back in place and looked over at Sammy Hyde.

"Who's going to get killed when they come to bust you out?" he said. His eyes were opened wide, and he was smiling. One of the Bartlet men stepped back into the room.

"They're both dead," he said.

"Go wake up Gool," said Tommy. "Tell him he's got another job to do."

"Okay, Tommy."

The gunshots did not wake up the town. No one came running to find out what had happened. Slocum was out cold on his hotel room floor. Except for the two dead Oates hands and the two on-duty Bartlet hands, everyone else was sleeping. If anyone heard the shots, no one thought much about them or gave a damn. It was well after sunup before anyone came around, and then it was Slocum checking in at the office. Everything seemed normal.

"Go on and get some sleep, Tommy," Slocum said.

"I got to tell you something first," Tommy said, glancing at the two Bartlet hands. "Two of Oates's men came around last night. They were going to try to bust Sammy out. I killed them."

"Both of them?"

"Yeah. Both of them."

"All right," Slocum said. "Go on now."

In another few minutes two more Bartlet hands came in to relieve the ones who had been on duty. Somehow they had already heard the news.

"It's a safe bet Oates and his bunch know about it by now," said Slocum.

"They'll be coming, won't they?" said one of the hands.

"Maybe," said Slocum.

"Come on, Slocum. You know they will."

"They will unless something happens first to stop them," Slocum said.

"Your deputy just blasted two of Oates's boys with a fucking shotgun," said one of the hands.

"Oates won't like it, but he won't do anything about it. His boys were trying to break Hyde out of jail."

"Slocum," said the taller and slimmer of the two ranch hands, "that ain't the way we heard it."

"What?"

"Well, you know, we had two hands in here last night when the shooting took place."

"I know that."

"They said them two fellows just opened the door. One of them said two words, but they wasn't enough to tell what they wanted. Neither one of them went for a gun. Hell, Slocum, they wasn't even wearing guns. Tommy just grabbed the shotgun and blasted away before anyone could've known what the hell they was up to."

"He never give them a chance," said the other one.

Slocum leaned forward. "Are you sure about that?"

"That's what our boys told us, and they wouldn't have no reason to lie about it. Hell, they was on the other side."

"Does Oates know this?" Slocum asked.

"I don't see how he could know it. Our boys never told him. No one else seen it."

"All right," Slocum said. "Keep it quiet. It might've been better if you hadn't told me."

He stood up and stomped out of the office, walking straight to Tommy Howard's room. Arriving at the front door, he kicked it open and tromped into the room. Tommy was asleep on a narrow cot, and at the noise, he sat up straight in bed. Slocum slapped him across the face.

"You dumb son of a bitch," he said. "What the hell did you do it for? Are you getting trigger happy or what?"

"You talking about them two I shot last night?"

"Who the hell else?"

"I told you about it. They came for Hyde."

"Did they say that?"

"No."

"Did they have guns in their hands?"

"Well, no, but they was going for them."

"You saw their hands going for their guns?"

"Well, hell, Slocum, there wasn't time."

"They were unarmed, you silly shit. Could it be they just wanted to talk to him? Maybe bring him some whiskey?"

"I don't think so. I don't see how—"

"Goddamn it, Tommy, I ought to fire you. Hell, I ought to lock you up in jail. But then folks would want to know why, and I can't tell them. If Oates finds out how it really happened, he'll start the shooting war for sure."

"He might start it anyhow, mightn't he?"

"Yeah. He might."

Tommy sat up and reached for his trousers.

"What the hell are you doing?" said Slocum. "Go back to sleep."

"I can't sleep now, Slocum. I might just as well get up and go back to the office."

"Suit yourself."

"Damn," Tommy said. "There ought to be some way to hold them off."

Then it came back to Slocum. It came from the depths of a woozy brain, from out of the mists of a groggy reality, from something like a foggy dream that had been lost but was just coming back, in and out, not quite clear. He looked around the room and found a chair, which he sat down on. Tommy was pulling on his boots.

"Something wrong, Slocum?" he said.

"Shut up, Tommy. Let me think."

By the time Tommy was dressed, Slocum's idea from the night before had come back clear. He knew what he wanted to do. He stood up, impatient.

"Come on, Tommy," he said. Tommy followed Slocum out of the house. They were walking in the general direction of the marshal's office. Slocum said, "Tommy, I want you to go see Bartlet. Tell him to have his whole damned outfit in the street in front of my office at one o'clock this afternoon."

"What for?"

"Just tell him what I told you. That's all."

As Tommy turned off toward the Fat Back saloon, Slocum headed on toward the office. Along the way, he met one of the Oates hands and stopped him there on the sidewalk.

"What you want, Marshal?" the man said.

"I want you to tell your boss," Slocum said, "to have

all of you boys out in the street in front of my office at one o'clock this afternoon."

"How come?" said the hand.

"Just tell him what I told you," said Slocum. "That's all."

"I don't know if he'll do it without some reason for it," the man said.

"Tell him what I said. That's all."

The cowboy scratched his head all the way back to the Fancy Pants saloon. When he went in, Oates was there with three other hands. Oates looked up as the hand approached him.

"Morning, Beck," he said.

"Boss," said Beck, "I just run into the marshal out on the street. He told me to tell you to be out on the street in front of his office at one o'clock this afternoon with all of us."

Oates wrinkled his nose in puzzlement. "How come?" he said.

"I asked him that, and he wouldn't say. Just said, 'Tell him what I said.' "

"That was it?"

"Yes, sir."

At just about that time, Tommy walked into the Fat Back. There were a couple of Bartlet's men in there, but there was no sign of Bartlet. "Good morning, Deputy," said one of the men. Tommy crossed the room to sit with the man and his two companions.

"Morning," he said. "I'm looking for Mr. Bartlet."

"He ain't showed up yet this morning, but I reckon he'll be along pretty soon."

"I'm supposed to give him a message from Slocum."

"Have a cup of coffee with us while you wait."

"Well, sure. Can't be no harm in that," Tommy said.

"We heard you nailed a couple of the Oates boys last night," said one of the Bartlet hands.

"Well, yeah. I did."

"They was trying to break out ole Hyde?"

"That's what it looked like to me."

"Good for you," said the cowboy. "That's two less for us to worry about."

"Hey," said another one, "here comes the boss."

Tommy looked over his shoulder to see Bartlet coming. He stood up to meet the man. "Good morning, sir," he said.

"Good morning, Deputy."

"Mr. Bartlet, Slocum sent me over here with a message for you."

"All right. What is it?"

"Slocum would like for you and all of your boys to be on the street in front of the jail at one o'clock this afternoon."

"Is that it?"

"Yes, sir."

"Did he say why?"

"No, sir."

"Well, all right. Tell him that we'll be there."

"Thank you, Mr. Bartlet," said Tommy, and he turned and left the saloon.

One of the cowboys looked up at Bartlet.

"What do you suppose that's all about, boss?" he asked.

Bartlet shrugged. "I don't know," he said.

"You want some coffee, boss?"

"Yes, I do," said Bartlet, pulling out a chair to sit in.

11

At twelve thirty, Slocum went into the Fat Back saloon and told the barkeep to gather up all of the guns that had been checked and haul them to the jail. He walked on to the Fancy Pants and gave the same instructions there. Then he walked back to his office. Tommy was there with the two Bartlet hands. Hyde was sulking in his cell. The two bartenders were there, loaded down with guns. A few minutes before one o'clock, Bartlet and his hands started gathering in the street. In another minute, Oates and his boys showed up. They stood facing each other, the dividing line being Slocum's office. Slocum said to the two Bartlet hands in the office, "Get out there in the street with your boss."

"What's up, Marshal?" one of them asked.

"Just get on out there." The two hands went outside, and Slocum stood up. He walked over to Charlie, the barkeep from the Fancy Pants. "Go out there now and pass those guns out to their owners," he said.

"What?" Charlie said.

"You heard me right," Slocum said. "Get going." Charlie went out the door, and Slocum turned to the other barkeep. "You, too," he said. "Same thing." The second bartender went on out with no questions, no comments.

Out on the street, the cowhands were looking confused. Oates said, "What the hell is this?" He got no answer. Slocum stepped out onto the sidewalk in front of his office and stood watching the distribution of the guns. When all the cowhands, as well as their two bosses, were armed once again, Slocum sent the barkeeps scampering back to their stations at their respective saloons. Both of them ran like hell. No one could tell if it was because of the street full of armed cowhands or because they were afraid someone back in the saloon might pour himself a free drink.

"All right," Slocum said in a loud and clear voice, "get after it."

It was incredibly quiet in Shit Creek just then.

"Well, go on," Slocum said. "Start to shooting."

A few hands went hesitatingly toward guns, but instead of hauling them out, their owners looked, puzzled, toward Slocum or toward their bosses, or both. Oates stepped out a few feet in front of his crew and looked at Slocum.

"Slocum," he called out, "what's the meaning of this?"

Bartlet stepped out next. "What the hell are you trying to pull here?"

"You two men have been itching to have a war with each other for some time, from what I've heard," Slocum said. "Then Sammy Hyde did you all a favor. He killed Bennie Dill. I believe that was the fellow's name. He gave you an excuse. Oates wants Sammy to get out of jail, get away with murder. Bartlet wants to see Sammy hang. Both of you came into town with your crews, ready to fight it out on the streets. Am I right?"

He looked at Oates, who did not answer him. He looked at Bartlet. "Am I right?" Still he got no answer.

"Well, then, get to killing. Here's your chance. We'll find out who the last man standing will be. We'll declare a winner. So pull your guns and start shooting now."

"Slocum," yelled Oates, "have you gone crazy?"

"I'm just giving you both what you've been yearning for. That's all."

"This ain't the way, Slocum," Bartlet said.

"What do you mean?" Slocum said. "Was I wrong? You don't want this?"

"We ain't going to stand here in the middle of the street and start shooting each other," said Oates.

"All right then," said Slocum. "Get your horses and get out of town. That's your only other option. And I mean right now."

Bartlet looked at Oates. Oates gave a nod.

"Let's go get our horses, boys," said Bartlet.

The Bartlet hands looked from their boss to the Oates hands facing them. They looked at one another. Bartlet was already walking toward the stable. His cowboys started to follow him.

"Let's go home, boys," said Oates, and his hands followed him. In another minute, the street was deserted except for Richard Cherry, who stood alone, staring at Slocum there on the sidewalk. He waited a few seconds, and then he walked up to stand in front of Slocum.

"That was a cute trick, Marshal," he said. "What if it hadn't worked?"

"Then we'd have a bunch of dead cowboys in the street," Slocum said. "The troubles would all be over."

"And what would have become of your job if you'd let a big fight like that go on in town?"

"It wouldn't matter. There wouldn't be no need for it."

"I guess you had it all figured out. So what happens now?"

"We'll have us a trial Monday morning."

"And then a hanging?"

"Most likely."

"I imagine Oates will have something to say about that. You'll be right back where you started. So what did all this gain you?"

"A little time, Cherry, that's all."

"Well, I guess I'll go down to the saloon and have myself a drink. You want to join me?"

"I don't mind," said Slocum.

They walked together to the Fat Back saloon and went inside. Cherry headed for the bar, but Slocum stopped him. He jerked a thumb toward the sign about checking guns. Cherry looked at it, shrugged, and unbuckled his belt, handing the guns across the bar to the barkeep. Slocum got a bottle and two glasses and went to a table. Cherry followed him and they both sat down. Slocum poured the drinks. They each took a swig.

"Slocum," Cherry said, "I sure am glad I ain't sitting in your chair."

"Yeah?"

"You got trouble coming. That's for sure."

"You going to be part of it?" Slocum said.

"I don't know what I'll be doing," Cherry said. "Not till the time comes. It would be interesting, though, you and me facing each other."

"You think so?"

"Don't you?"

"I suppose so, to some bystander."

"The way you talk," Cherry said, "someone might think that you're scared of facing me."

"I might be," said Slocum.

Cherry laughed and took another drink.

"I can't figure you, Cherry," Slocum said. "How do you fit in with this fucking mess?"

Cherry shrugged. "It's a job," he said. "We all got to eat. And it ain't no worse than what you're doing."

God, Slocum thought, he's right about that, for sure. He was embarrassed again about his predicament. He had told himself that he was on the side of the law in this situation, but he wasn't real certain about that. Oh, Hyde was guilty, for sure, but Hyde was just an excuse for a range war that had been about to flare up for a long time. So Cherry had signed on with Oates, and Slocum had signed on with Bartlet. What the hell was the difference? Was Bartlet any better than Oates? Slocum had no idea.

Just then, a saloon gal came walking into the room. Slocum suddenly realized that he had not seen any saloon gals in all the days he had been in Shit Creek. She walked over to the table where he and Cherry were seated.

"You want some company?" she asked.

"Sit down," Cherry said. Then he raised his voice. "Barkeep, bring another glass, will you?"

"Sure thing."

The gal sat down next to Cherry.

"Where you been the last few days?" Slocum asked.

"Hiding out," the gal said. "We thought there was fixing to be a shooting war."

The barkeep brought the glass and put it on the table. Slocum poured whiskey in it, and the gal took it up and had a sip.

"Are there others?" said Slocum.

"Two more here," she said.

"In the other saloon?"

"I think there're four over there."

"Well, I'll be damned."

"Forget all that," said Cherry. "What's your name, sweet thing?"

"Amanda," she said.

"Well, my name's Richard Cherry. You can call me Cherry. This grumpy ole fart over here is your new marshal. His name's Slocum."

"Well," said Amanda, "I'm pleased to meet the both of you."

Slocum tipped his hat.

"Likewise, Amanda," said Cherry.

"I haven't seen you around before," she said.

"He rode in while you were in hiding," said Slocum.

Cherry laughed. "Yeah. He's right about that."

"You going to be around here for long?" she asked.

Cherry shrugged. "Oh, that depends on how long the job lasts," he said.

Amanda looked across the table at Slocum. "What about you?" she said.

"Same answer," said Slocum. "When the job's done, I'm done."

"Are you two working together?"

"We were just talking about that before you came in," Cherry said. "We just might be gunning for each other before it's all over with."

Amanda looked from Slocum to Cherry and back with astonishment, but before she could think of anything to say, Slocum stood up. "I better be headed back to the office," he said, and he left the saloon without another word. Cherry watched him go. Amanda turned her head to watch him. Then she looked back at Cherry.

"He's a strange one," she said.

"I'd have said 'interesting,'" Cherry said, "but 'strange' will do."

"Are you really going to try to kill him?"

Cherry gave a shrug. "I can't tell for sure. It depends on how this feud between Oates and Bartlet turns out. Oates wants to get Sammy Hyde out of jail and keep him from hanging, and I'm working for Oates. Bartlet wants to see Hyde strung up. Slocum's the town marshal. We're kind of stuck in the middle."

"I see," said Amanda. "Sort of."

"Don't let it worry you," said Cherry with a wide grin. "Probably won't nothing happen till Monday morning, anyway."

Amanda put a hand on one of Cherry's hands. He made no objection. "You want to go upstairs with me?" she asked.

"Right now," he said, "there ain't nothing I'd rather do."

She stood up and pulled on his hand. "Well, let's go then," she said.

Cherry stood and picked up the bottle and the two glasses and allowed her to tug him along to the bottom of the stairs. Then they climbed the stairs together. At the top, she led him about halfway down the hall and opened a door. She stepped into the room and waited for him to enter. He did so, looked around, then put the bottle and glasses down on a small table. She shut the door and latched it. She moved to the bed and started to undress herself. Cherry took the hint and started to do the same thing.

In another minute, they were standing naked, looking at each other. She held out her arms, and Cherry
walked into them. They embraced and kissed, and his
hands slid down to her butt, one hand catching one
round side and the other catching its twin. She pressed
herself against him, mashing her breasts against his
chest. After a few seconds, they parted, and she crawled
onto the bed on her hands and knees, her round ass
flashing at him for a few seconds. When she reached the
middle of the mattress, she rolled over on her back and
spread her legs, smiling and reaching out for him.

He moved in and lay on top of her. He kissed her
again while his hand felt her breast. Her hands moved
between their bodies to search for his crotch. She found
his tool long and hard and ready for action. She
squeezed it, and it bucked and jumped in her hand.

"Oh," she said. "That's ready to go."

"It damn sure is," said Cherry.

She guided the head into her slit and rubbed it up and
down between the wet and slippery lips, and then she
found her hole with it and aimed it in the right direction.
Cherry thrust forward and went in deep. At the same
time, Amanda pushed her hips upward to meet his
thrust. Together, they pumped again and again. Then
they started driving hard and fast.

"Oh. Oh. Oh."

12

Out at the Simple Simon Ranch, Simon Oates had called in Mo Diamond and Richard Cherry. They sat together around a big dining-room table in Oates's huge ranch house. Oates had put out three glasses, and he brought out his best bottle of French brandy. After inviting the other two men to sit down, Oates poured brandy all around. Then he sat. He lifted his glass. The other two lifted theirs. Then they each took a first sip.

"That's fine stuff, Mr. Oates," said Cherry.

"I always try to buy the best," Oates said.

"That ain't why you called us in here, boss," said Diamond, who was always practical.

"You're right, Mo," Oates said. "We got some serious business to consider. Today is Saturday. They're trying Sammy on Monday morning. Our time is short. We have today and tomorrow."

"You still meaning to try to break Sammy out of jail?" asked Diamond.

"I've never wavered from my original intentions," said Oates. "He's a young fool, but he's one of my boys."

"Mr. Oates," Diamond said, "you know that Sammy

is guilty as hell. There were plenty of witnesses that seen him go get his gun and shoot that man down. The other man was unarmed."

"I know that, Mo. I know it. But I always back up my boys, and even if I didn't, I've already said it out loud in front of the whole town. I can't back down now. Every saddle bum around will think he can take advantage of me."

"So what do you mean to do?" asked Diamond. "Raid the jailhouse? You tried that once before."

"If Slocum were out of the way," Oates said, "there would be no problem."

He gave Cherry an unmistakable look.

"You, uh, want me to—"

"There would be five hundred dollars in it for you," Oates said.

Diamond stood up, leaving most of a glass of brandy on the table. "I didn't hear any of that," he said. "I have a ranch to run."

"Then get back to your job, Mo," said Oates. "Or better yet, pack up your gear and get out. If you don't have the same feeling for the boys as I have, I don't need you."

Diamond stopped and looked at Oates for a moment. Oates stared hard back at him, seemingly unfeeling. Diamond thought that he had always known Oates was a hard old man, but he had never before realized just how hard, how stone-headed, the old son of a bitch was. He turned and walked out of the room without another word. Oates turned back to Cherry.

"When will you do it?" he asked.

"I'll have to pick the right time," Cherry said. "And you know, I never do a murder. I always give a man a chance. I'll have to goad Slocum into a fight, and there's always a chance that he'll come out on top."

"I want him dead," said Oates.

"You heard my terms."

"All right. All right. Then go ahead. Get after it."

Cherry downed his remaining brandy. He stood up and touched the brim of his hat. "I'll be in touch, Mr. Oates," he said, and he walked out the door. Oates swallowed the rest of his brandy and poured himself another. Once Slocum is dead, he thought, I'll take a few of the boys into town, and we'll let Sammy out of jail. Without Slocum, no one will dare try to stop us.

Outside, Richard Cherry threw a saddle on his horse and tied his blanket roll on behind the saddle. He mounted up and rode casually toward Shot Creek.

Slocum stepped into the marshal's office, and Tommy Howard, who was sitting behind the big desk fondling his shotgun, jumped up to move and make room for his boss.

"Stay there, Tommy," Slocum said. "You enjoy that pompous fucking desk more than I do."

Tommy, sheepishly, sat back down. He placed the shotgun on the desk in front of him.

"What's up, Slocum?" he asked.

"Not much. How've things been in here?"

"Quiet," said Tommy, "except for ole Sammy in there trying to beg his way out of jail."

Slocum shot a glance at Sammy Hyde, who looked down at the floor to avoid Slocum's gaze.

"You'd best hope that Tommy don't let you out of there, Sammy," Slocum said, "'cause if he did, I'd have to hunt you down and shoot you."

"Be better than hanging," Sammy mumbled.

Slocum walked over to the cell door and leaned on it, looking in at the prisoner.

"You know, Sammy," he said, "I'll be glad to see you hang. Anyone chickenshit enough to grab a gun and shoot down an unarmed man just because he was getting whipped in a fistfight ain't worth the price of a bullet."

Sammy turned to the wall and kept quiet. Slocum walked over and sat on the front edge of the big desk.

"I'll be damn glad when Monday morning comes and goes," he said. "I'll be damn glad when this hanging's over with."

"Yeah?" said Tommy. "What'll you do then? Ride out of here? Just like that?"

"You're goddamned right, boy," Slocum said.

"Where'll you go?"

"There's other towns."

"What'll you do for a job? You can't find a better job than what you got here. The pay's good, and you don't have to buy nothing. You can save all your money. And you don't even have to work for it. You got me to do all the work."

"I guess I just ain't too bright," Slocum said.

"I'd say it's being bright," said Hyde. "Be even brighter if you was to scoot out of town right now."

"Well, Sammy, you little shit," Slocum said, "for once I agree with you."

Sammy jumped up off his cot and moved quickly over to the cell door. He grasped the bars with both hands and looked out wide-eyed and hopeful at Slocum. "So you leaving then?" he asked.

"Like I told Tommy," Slocum said, "I ain't too bright."

"Shit," said Hyde.

"You just leave everything to me, old man," said Tommy. "I'll take care of them for you." He patted his shotgun and smiled.

Slocum's lips twisted. He couldn't stand another minute of these two young snots. He headed for the door. "I'm going for some coffee," he said.

"I can make a pot," said Tommy.

"Like I said, I'm going for some coffee."

He left the office and headed for the eatery. He figured he'd find Terri Sue at work there. If she wasn't too busy, she would make better company than those two back in the jailhouse. He wondered when things were going to come to a head. How soon would Oates make his move, and what would that move be? He knew that the old fart was not going to give it up—something was going to happen. There wasn't much time left.

He walked into the eating place and found Terri Sue waiting on tables. There were three tables occupied. One of them was occupied by Mayor Will Church and Councilman Mike Fall. Slocum headed for an empty table, but Church intercepted him.

"Join us, Slocum," he said.

"I don't want to butt in on nothing," Slocum said.

"No. Please," the mayor said.

Slocum pulled out a chair and sat. Terri Sue had caught sight of him and brought him a cup of coffee. "Thanks," he said.

She smiled down at him and said, "Sure thing, cowboy."

"How're things going, Marshal Slocum?" the councilman said.

"Creeping along," said Slocum.

"Anything resolved?"

"It will be soon," Slocum said. "I'd say Monday morning for sure."

"You got all those cowboys out of town," said Church.

"Yeah. It just makes things seem more peaceful for the time being," Slocum said. "They're still boiling, though. They'll boil over sometime between now and Monday morning."

"Are you sure of that?" said Fall.

"Ain't you? Oates ain't going to just let this go. Not now. He's got a reputation to save. He's also got a new hired gun out at his place."

"That Cherry?" said Church.

"That's him. Richard Cherry." Slocum sipped some coffee. It was hot, and it was good.

"Do you suppose," said Church, "that you'll have to face Cherry?"

"I'll be surprised if I don't," Slocum said. "You don't hire a man like Cherry just for show."

"We have confidence in you, Slocum," Church said.

"I hate to say it," said Slocum, "but I have more confidence in Tommy and his shotgun. It don't miss."

"Slocum," said Church, "do you need more deputies? We can hire as many as you need—temporarily, of course."

"We've already got two armies fixing to face each other in this town," Slocum said. "I don't think we need another one. Thanks just the same."

"All right. It's your—"

"Funeral?"

"I was going to say, 'It's your show.'"

"Yeah."

The front door opened and Richard Cherry walked

in. He tipped his hat to Terri Sue and walked to the table where the three men were sitting. "Gentlemen," he said.

"Mr. Cherry, is it?" said Church.

"That's me. Now you got the advantage on me."

"I'm Will Church, the mayor of Shot Creek. This is Mike Fall, one of our councilmen."

"How do," said Cherry. "Now that we've been properly introduced, reckon I can sit down."

"You haven't been invited," said Fall.

"I'm inviting him," said Slocum. "Unless you want me to move."

"Sit down, Mr. Cherry," said Church.

Cherry looked at Fall, pulled out a chair, and sat down directly across the table from Slocum. "Thanks," he said.

Terri Sue came over with a fresh cup of coffee and put it down in front of Cherry. He looked up at her and smiled. "And thank you, pretty lady," he said. "Are you spoke for?"

Terri Sue looked at Slocum. His expression was noncommittal. "No," she said. "I'm not."

"That's nice to know," said Cherry. He picked up his coffee and took a sip. "Ouch. It's hot."

"That's the way most people like it," she said.

Cherry laughed as Terri Sue walked away to tend to business.

"So what brings you to town, Mr. Cherry?" Church asked.

"That cook out at Simple Simon Ranch don't make good coffee," Cherry said.

"You rode all the way in just for a good cup of coffee?"

"A really good cup of coffee is worth a long ride," Slocum said. "Ain't it, Cherry?"

"Sure is. You notice, Slocum, I'm wearing my guns."

"I saw that."

"No problem?"

"You can wear them anywhere you want in Shit Creek," Slocum said, "except in the saloons."

"Except in saloons," Cherry echoed.

"That's where the trouble usually starts."

"Usually," said Cherry. "But not always."

"Is this conversation going somewhere?" asked Fall.

"Oh, I don't know," Cherry said. "Just making small talk. Trying to be friendly."

"I think Cherry here came into town to kill me," Slocum said.

Church and Fall stiffened. Cherry put down his coffee cup and looked into Slocum's eyes.

"Now what made you say that?" he asked.

"Experience. Am I right?"

"You're all of a sudden worth five hundred dollars to me," Cherry said. "Dead, of course."

"Of course."

"But you have to cooperate with me."

"Oh?"

"I never gun a man who didn't draw on me first."

"You've got a problem then," Slocum said. "I won't do that."

13

Slocum walked into the Fat Back saloon to get a drink and to look around. He noticed right away that no one was wearing a gun. Except for the smoldering range war, things appeared to have settled down in Shot Creek. He walked to the bar and stood next to a cowhand. When he got beside the man, he recognized him. He had only seen him once, the first time he had seen Oates, at the jail. The man noticed Slocum at the same time.

"Howdy, Marshal," the man said.

"I recognize you," Slocum said, "but I don't know if I ever got your name."

"It's Mo Diamond."

"You work for Oates," said Slocum.

"I was his foreman," said Diamond. "He fired me."

"Oh, yeah? What for?"

"On account of I wasn't so eager as him to break Sammy Hyde out of jail."

"I see. So he's still planning on that, is he?"

"He don't mean to see Sammy hang, if that's what you're getting at. But that's all I know. Even if I did know more, I wouldn't say anything about it. He fired my ass, but I worked for him for a good long time, and I still got some loyalty toward him."

"Well, I can't fault you for that. What are you planning to do?"

Diamond shrugged. "I got no plans. Ain't in a hurry. I saved up a little money over the years. I'll just hang around here awhile till I figure it out."

"Mo, let me buy you a drink." Slocum could afford to be generous with the town paying all his bills.

"Why not?" said Diamond. "Thanks."

Slocum got a bottle and the two men sat down at a table. Slocum poured two drinks.

"There ain't many who'd give up a good job like you did on a matter of principle," Slocum said.

"It don't seem like too much," Diamond said. "A man who won't stand up for what he believes in ain't worth a damn, the way I see it."

Just then, Richard Cherry walked in. He grinned, took off his gunbelt and handed it to the barkeep, and then walked directly to the table where Slocum and Diamond were seated.

"Mind if I sit down, gents?" he said. Not waiting for a response, he pulled out a chair and sat. He waved a hand at the barkeep for another glass.

"I guess not," Slocum said.

"Buy me a drink, Slocum?" Cherry said. Then he reached for the bottle and, when the barkeep put down the glass, poured it full.

Cherry turned up the glass and drank about half of its contents in a gulp. He put the glass back down and looked at Diamond. "The marshal here won't fight me," he said. "He told me as much."

"Seems like a right smart attitude," said Diamond.

"Seems a little cowardly to me," said Cherry.

"I was raised to avoid a fight if it's possible," said Diamond.

"Well, I guess it takes all kinds," said Cherry. "Still, I wouldn't want a man like that for a town marshal. Not when there's trouble brewing."

"What kind of trouble are you looking for, Cherry?" asked Slocum.

"Hell, you know as well as I do."

"I ain't the one who's got a special place with the man who might be fixing to start the trouble," Slocum said.

"You mean Mr. Oates?" said Cherry. "He don't want no trouble."

"Not much," said Slocum. "He just wants you to kill me for him, and then he means to bust Sammy Hyde out of jail."

"That's what I mean. With you dead, it won't be no trouble at all to get Sammy out of jail. Oates don't want trouble. See?"

"He'll have trouble if Slocum here won't cooperate with you," said Diamond.

Cherry drained the rest of the liquid from his glass and poured himself another. "I never knew a man to just sit by when someone else drank his whiskey without being invited," he said.

"Drink all you want," said Slocum.

"I will," Cherry said.

"I'd be just tickled to see you staggering drunk," Slocum said.

"Don't hold your breath. I can hold my liquor pretty good. Have another?"

"I've had enough," Slocum said. He watched Cherry

down the drink he was holding and then pour another. Slocum stood up and took off his own gunbelt. He walked over to the bar and handed it to the barkeep. Then he walked back to the table and looked down at Cherry. "So you want to fight me," he said.

Cherry looked up at him with a surprised expression. "You know what I meant," he said.

Slocum said, "You like my whiskey? Have another." He picked up the drink Cherry had poured himself and tossed it in Cherry's face. Cherry was on his feet instantly.

"Damn it," he said.

"You want a fight?" said Slocum, slapping Cherry in the face. "Come on."

"Let's get our guns and go out in the street," Cherry said.

Slocum grabbed Cherry's shirt front and shoved him toward the door. "We don't need guns to go out in the street," he said. He shoved Cherry backward through the batwing door, and Cherry sprawled on his back in the dirt street. He rolled over quickly and scrambled to his feet, staring at Slocum, who was still up on the sidewalk.

"You son of a bitch," he said.

"You still plan on waiting for me to draw first?" Slocum asked.

"I'll kill you," said Cherry.

"You didn't answer my question."

"Get our guns."

"If you mean to stay out of the saloon," Slocum said, "you can get yours. Anytime."

"If I get my gun, I'll kill you."

"If I'm unarmed? In front of witnesses?"

Cherry started shaking in his anger.

"Get our guns," he said in a low and menacing voice.

"I don't mean to strap mine on," Slocum said. "I already told you, you can get yours and leave town."

"All right," said Cherry. "All right. I will."

He walked tentatively toward Slocum, who was blocking the doorway. It took three steps to reach the sidewalk, then one more to get up on the sidewalk. He was standing face-to-face with Slocum. Slocum stepped aside. Cherry went on in.

"Give me my guns," he said to the barkeep.

"You leaving us?"

"Hell yes. Give them to me."

The barkeep turned around and took Cherry's two-gun rig off the rack. He held it out toward Cherry, who grabbed it and stormed out the door, past Slocum, and out into the street, where he started strapping the rig on around his waist. Back inside the saloon, Diamond had gotten up and walked to the bar. Without a word, he pointed to his own gun. The barkeep handed it to him. He strapped it on, pulled out the gun, and stepped out onto the sidewalk.

Just then, Cherry jerked out one of his two shiny Colts, but before he could bring it into play against Slocum, Diamond raised his and fired. His bullet struck Cherry in the chest, just about at the heart. Cherry staggered back and looked down at the hole in his chest spurting blood. He looked up again at Slocum, who was still unarmed. His eyes widened. His fingers went limp, and he dropped the Colt to the ground. His knees went weak and he staggered two steps. Then his knees buckled, and Cherry fell on his face and did not move again.

Slocum looked at Diamond. "You just dealt yourself a hand in this game," he said.

"I could tell he was fixing to abandon his rule," Diamond said. "He'd have shot you, even unarmed. You had him real pissed off, Marshal."

"Yeah. I reckon I did."

Diamond holstered his gun and went back into the saloon, where he turned it in again and went back to the table. Slocum stood on the sidewalk until he saw Tommy running toward him, holding the shotgun. When Tommy got closer, Slocum said, "You don't need that Greener, boy. You're a little too late."

Tommy stopped running and looked down at the body of Cherry in the street. "That's Cherry," he said.

"That's obvious," said Slocum. "Take care of it, will you?"

"Yeah. Sure." Tommy looked at Slocum and saw that he was not wearing his gun. "Slocum?" he said. "Marshal?"

But Slocum had turned and walked into the Fat Back. He returned to the table with Mo Diamond and sat down. Reaching for the bottle, he poured another drink.

"I hope it's all right that I already poured myself one," said Diamond.

"It sure is," said Slocum.

Tommy Howard came into the saloon and walked over to the table.

"Slocum?" he said.

"What is it?"

"You-you weren't wearing a gun."

"Is that right?"

"So how did you—Who—"

"Tommy," said Slocum, "I gave you a job to do."

"Yes, sir," said Tommy, and he turned and hurried out the door.

Slocum took a sip of his drink. He looked at Diamond.

"Mo," he said, "I could use another deputy."

"Not me, Slocum," Diamond said.

"Why not?"

"I told you already," said Diamond. "I won't go against Oates."

"Hell," said Slocum. "You just did."

"I didn't go against Oates," said Diamond. "I just seen a man about to do a murder, and I stopped him. That's all."

"He was about to do what he was about to do for Oates," Slocum said. "It was his job. He was going to get five hundred bucks from Oates for it."

"Forget it, Slocum. I don't want a job."

"All right," Slocum said. "Suit yourself. But thanks for what you did anyhow."

Slocum got up, retrieved his gun, and headed for the office. He found Tommy sitting behind the big desk, fondling his shotgun, and Sammy Hyde sulking in the cell. "What's up?" he said.

"Nothing's up in here," said Tommy. "You had all the excitement today. Getting that two-gun gunfighter killed like that. How did you do it, Slocum?"

"I didn't do it, Tommy. You saw me. I had no gun."

"Well, are you going to tell me what happened?"

"Mo Diamond shot him, Tommy. By the time you came running up, he'd gone back inside and turned his gun in again. Mo shot him because he was about to gun me, and I was unarmed."

"Mo Diamond?" said Tommy.

"What are you talking about?" Sammy Hyde almost shouted from the cell. "Diamond works for Mr. Oates. You're lying."

"Oates fired Diamond," Slocum said.

"Bullshit," said Hyde. "You're lying."

"You shut up, Hyde," said Slocum. "I wasn't talking to you anyhow."

Hyde recalled the abrupt bath he'd had earlier and decided to shut up.

"When will they be coming, Slocum?" said Tommy.

"Hell, how should I know? They could come today or tomorrow. Or they could surprise us all and wait till the trial's over. If Sammy gets the noose, they might hit us then, before the hanging. There's no way to tell."

"I wish they'd go ahead and make their move. I wish they'd hurry up," Tommy said.

"Don't let it get to you, Tommy. That's all part of the plan. The longer they make us wait, the more nervous we get. Don't fall into their trap."

Hyde couldn't hold his tongue any longer. "Tommy's nervous, all right," he said. "And he's got some more waiting to do. He'll get more nervous. Might shit in his pants."

"Shut up," Tommy shouted, and he stood up and pointed the shotgun toward the cell. Sammy shrank into a corner, huddled up, frightened.

"Calm down, Tommy," Slocum said.

"I ought to blast your ass," Tommy said to Hyde. "I ought to splatter you all over that cell."

He walked back to the desk and put the shotgun down on top of it. Then he dropped back into the chair.

"You know what, Sammy?" he said. Sammy, still quivering in the corner, did not answer. "However long we have to wait, you have the same wait that I do."

14

Bartlet called all of his men together in front of his ranch house. He stood on the porch facing them. "Boys," he called out. "Hold it down." They grew quiet. It was Saturday, late afternoon. "All right. Listen to me. The time is almost here. The trial is set for Monday morning.

"You all know Oates's attitude. He wants Hyde out of jail. Wants to set him free. Sammy Hyde gunned down Bennie Dill when Bennie wasn't even wearing a gun. Murdered him in cold blood. I mean to see that trial go forth. I mean to see Bennie's killer get what's coming to him, and that's a rope."

The cowhands all agreed loudly. Bartlet held up his hands for quiet. Soon they calmed down and listened again.

"I think Oates might try to pull something. There's only two lawmen in Shot Creek. One of them's got to sleep. Now, we can't be sure when Oates will try to pull something. There are several possibilities, and the first one is that he'll try something before the trial. He could try tonight. I want two of you boys to volunteer to ride out and watch the Simple Simon. If you see anyone heading for town, hurry back here and let the rest of us know."

"I'll go, boss," shouted a cowhand who was standing up front.

"All right, Jesse," said Bartlet.

"Here, boss," called another.

"Good," said Bartlet. "Jesse, you and Levi saddle up and head out. Remember now: I don't want no shooting. Just watch, and get back here if you see any movement."

"Gotcha, boss," said Jesse.

Jesse and Levi hurried away from the general gathering. Bartlet stood for a moment and watched them go.

"All right now," said Bartlet, "the rest of you be ready to jump and run if those boys report back to us any movement over at the Simple Simon.

"If they don't make a move now, they'll make it later. They might wait to see how the trial comes out, and if Hyde is sentenced to hang, they'll move before the hanging date. We can't know. We just have to stay ready. We have to keep our eyes open. That's all."

Just then Jesse and Levi rode by, heading for the front gate. At the gate, they turned toward the Simple Simon Ranch. They rode hard for a time. Then they slowed their horses to an easy pace. They passed no one on the road, so when they reached the main gate to the Simple Simon, they looked around for a good place from which to keep watch. Across the road from the gate, the land rose up several feet. The slight rise was covered in brush and small boulders. Immediately across from the gate, it was too steep to climb, but not far down the road, they located a place where they could manage.

"Let's try this, Levi," said Jesse.

"Okay."

They turned their mounts and headed up the rise. When they reached the top, they looked around. They had a clear view of the gate and much of the road.

"This works," said Levi.

"We can see down there, but they can't see us up here. Except for the horses, maybe."

They both turned in their saddles and looked around. There was room behind them to secure the horses so they would be out of sight from below. They did that and moved back to the front, selecting places to settle. Levi found a spot behind a small boulder. Jesse slouched down behind a clump of brush. They settled in for a long wait.

From where they watched, they could not see the Oates ranch house, but if they could have, they would have seen that the lights were still on. Oates was awake, and he had two of his cowhands in the house with him. He poured three glasses of brandy and settled himself and the two hands in comfortable chairs.

"Boys," he said, "I don't know what Slocum or Bartlet expects of us. But one thing is for sure. We ain't going in there again like a fucking army. We tried that once, and it didn't work."

"No, sir, it didn't," said one of the hands.

"We ain't waiting to see Sammy tried and found guilty, though," Oates went on. "I called you two in for a reason. I want two men I can trust—"

"Hell, boss," said the other cowboy, "you can trust every one of your crew."

"I know that, Jordy," said Oates. "Let me finish."

"Sure, boss," Jordy said.

"I need two men I can trust with a special job. Two

men who can ride into town in the middle of the night unnoticed. Those same two men can likely get themselves into the jail some way."

Jordy and the other hand looked at one another, then back at their boss. Oates went on.

"I don't want anybody killed. Not unless there's no other way. You understand? I just want Sammy Hyde out of there. That's all."

"Leave it to us, boss," Jordy said.

"We'll get the job done," said the other cowboy.

"Thanks, Murv," said Oates. "You boys wait a few hours. Let it get well into the night before you head in. I don't want anybody to be expecting anything."

But Slocum was expecting trouble. He had gone to the jail to join Tommy. As usual, Tommy was behind the big desk. As usual, the shotgun was on the desktop in front of him. Slocum paced the floor.

"You're nervous, Slocum," Tommy said.

"Yeah. Ain't you?"

"Hell, no," Tommy said. He patted the shotgun and smiled. "This right here is the real equalizer. I can face down a whole crowd with this. I can take out three or four men with one shot."

"Yeah. Sure."

"I have two shots. I could take out eight men or so with them."

"That's if they're standing in a clump."

Tommy laughed. "Well, they don't scare me none. No, sir. They can ride in any time."

About that time, Jordy and Murv were riding out the main gate, leaving the Simple Simon. Up on the hill, Levi slapped Jesse on the shoulder. Jesse looked up. Levi and Jesse looked at one another.

"Two men," said Jesse.

"They're headed for town, looks like," Levi said.

"Will they try anything, just the two of them, you think?"

"I don't know, but all we're supposed to do is to tell the boss. That's all."

"Hey," said Jesse, "why don't you ride on back and report to him? I'll stay here and watch, in case there's any more movement, you know."

"Yeah," said Levi. "I'll do that."

He turned and ran back to his horse. He mounted up and rode down to the road and headed for the Bartlet ranch as fast as he could make the horse go. Up ahead of him, Jordy and Murv were moving steadily toward town.

In the marshal's office, Slocum excused himself. Leaving Tommy and his shotgun at the jail, he walked back to his hotel room. When he got there, he did not undress. He did not lie down on the bed. He pulled a chair over by the open window and sat where he had a good, clear view of the jail. His Winchester rifle was leaning on the wall beside him.

Levi rode hard up to the front porch of the Bartlet ranch house. He dismounted even before the horse had stopped, and he ran up onto the porch and pounded on the door. In a moment, Bartlet opened the door.

"Levi," he said. "What's up?"

"Two men rode out of Oates's place," he said. "They're headed for town."

"Just two?" asked Bartlet.

"Yes, sir. Just the two. Jesse stayed out there in case anything else happens."

"Good thinking," said Bartlet. "Get over to the bunkhouse and roust out about four of the boys. Send them right over here. Then you ride back and join Jesse again."

Bartlet's four men were on the road shortly, but the Oates hands had a head start on them. However, Jordy and Murv, the Oates hands, were moving casually. They had no idea they were being followed. The four Bartlet riders were moving fast. In spite of that, Jordy and Murv arrived first. They paused when they rode into Shot Creek.

"We got a plan?" Murv asked.

"Why don't you ride around to the back. I'll go to the front door. I'll knock. When you hear me, you come in the back door. Soon as you get the drop on whoever is in there, I'll come in."

"Why ain't you going in first?" asked Murv.

"The last time our boys went to the front door," Jordy said, "that deputy blasted them with his fucking shot-gun. I'm going to knock and then step aside. Wait for you."

"I get it. Okay. Let's do it."

They split up and rode on to the marshal's office, Murv taking the back route to the rear door. Jordy tied his horse to the rail in front and walked up on the sidewalk. He pulled out his six-gun and looked up and down the street. There was no one in sight. Using the butt of his gun, he rapped on the door. Around back, Murv heard the knocking. He tried the door and found it locked.

"Damn," he said.

Inside the jailhouse, Tommy stiffened and picked up the shotgun.

"Who is it?" he called out.

"Open up," Jordy yelled.

"I said who is it."

Across the street, Slocum raised his Winchester to his shoulder. "You down there," he called out. "Drop your gun."

Jordy looked over his shoulder, surprised. He held out the gun and was about to drop it when Bartlet's four men came riding into town. Seeing the Oates man in front of the jail with a gun in his hand, they opened fire. Jordy was hit by at least four bullets. He fell against the wall and slid slowly down to the sidewalk—dead.

Behind the jail, Murv heard the shots. He had heard Slocum's voice. He decided to keep quiet. As the four Bartlet riders came up in front of the jail, Slocum yelled again.

"You four shuck your irons," he called out. "This is Slocum talking."

The four looked at one another. They dropped their guns. About then, Tommy opened the front door and stepped out onto the sidewalk with his shotgun.

"Hold them there, Tommy," Slocum said. "I'm coming down."

Behind the jail, Murv huddled in the darkness, listening, trying to hear what was said. Slocum got to the jail, and Tommy was holding the shotgun on the four riders. "You got nothing on us, Marshal," said one of the four. "We rode in here and seen that fellow with a gun in his hand standing outside the jailhouse."

"That's right, Slocum," Tommy said. "He knocked on the door and yelled at me to open up. He wouldn't identify himself."

"It was an Oates man trying to break Hyde out of jail," said one of the riders.

"I saw him and heard him from upstairs," Slocum said to the riders. "Tommy was inside with a shotgun, and I had my Winchester on him. We didn't need any help from you boys."

"We didn't know that."

"What you did know," said Slocum, "is that there's law in Shit Creek. We don't need you or anyone else riding in here with your guns to try to take the law into your own hands. Get down off your horses."

"What are you fixing to do, Slocum?" asked one of the four.

"Get down."

The four riders dismounted.

"March inside," Slocum said.

The riders went inside the office, and Slocum followed them in. He got the keys off the desk and opened the cell next to Sammy's. He gestured toward the inside of the cell. "Get in there," he said.

"You ain't arresting us for preventing a jail break, are you?" asked one of the four.

"Get in," Slocum said.

The four men went into the cell, and Slocum shut and locked the door. He lowered his rifle and tossed the keys onto the desk.

"What's the charge?" one of them asked.

"Unauthorized killing," Slocum said. It was the first thing that popped into his head. Tommy walked up to Slocum and spoke in a low voice.

"Slocum," he said, "I believe they're right. That man they killed meant to break Sammy out of jail. I'm sure of it."

"I am, too," Slocum said. "That don't mean they had a

right to ride in here shooting. They stay in jail till Monday morning."

"What then?" asked one of the four.

"You'll get a trial."

Behind the jail, Murv crept over to his horse. He mounted up slowly, turned the animal, and started riding out of town inconspicuously. He had a lot to report to Mr. Oates.

15

Oates was really pissed off. Not only had his cowboys failed in their mission, but one of them had gotten himself killed. He was pissed off at the two cowboys, even the dead one, for having failed him. He was pissed off at Slocum and at Tommy Howard, just because. But he was really pissed off at Bartlet and his boys. He had been pissed off at Bartlet for a long time, but he was more pissed off than ever at the old bastard.

But now he had an added dimension to his already complex situation. He had a man in jail awaiting trial for the murder of one of Bartlet's hands, and now Bartlet had four men in jail for the killing of one of his men. He wondered if he should just wait for the trial, or trials, and see what happened. If the Bartlet hands should hang for their killing of Jordy, then it might balance out if Sammy Hyde was to hang for the killing of Bennie Dill. It might. He wasn't sure.

He was not at all sure that the Bartlet gang would hang, though. From what he had heard, he was surprised that Slocum had not patted them on the backs for their deed. Jordy was caught outside the jail with a gun in his hand in the middle of the night. And Slocum had, up until the day he had run them all out of town, used the Bartlet boys for jail guards. What they did might be seen as justified. Likely they would be turned loose and Sammy hanged. If he let it happen.

He wasn't at all sure what to do. His curiosity told him to wait for the trial. He did wonder what the judge, the goddamned mayor, would do with Sammy and then with the Bartlet men. He wondered if it would all balance out. And then, what difference would it make in the final analysis if he were to wait for the trial?

Things had gotten to the point that the only thing left for Oates to do was to ride into Shot Creek with his whole crew and blast the shit out of the town and rescue Sammy that way. That could be done after the trial as well as before. It was already Sunday, and the trial would go on tomorrow morning if he let the situation alone. They never hanged a man right after the trial. They set a day for the execution. He would still have time. He decided that he would wait.

Having made that decision, he mulled over some more thoughts. He was also pissed off at Mo Diamond. He expected absolute loyalty from his employees and felt that Mo had deserted him in a time of desperate need. He thought about Mo lounging around Shot Creek, drinking in the saloons, perhaps chatting with Slocum, maybe even planning on helping to defend the jailhouse from Oates's raid. Everyone knew that Oates would make a raid. They just did not know when it would come. He hoped that Diamond would help Slocum when the time came. He hoped that Diamond would get his ass shot to death. He was really pissed off.

And Bartlet was just about as riled. He had four men in jail now, and for what? For helping out the marshal? It did not make any sense to Bartlet. Slocum had come to Bartlet for help, and he had used Bartlet's men at the jail to help guard the prisoner. Now that Bartlet's cowhands had made a special trip to town in the middle of the night to help out, and they had come on a man outside the jail with a gun in his hand and killed him, Slocum had gotten all high and mighty and thrown them in jail. How were they to know that he was perched in a hotel window with a Winchester? According to Bartlet's reasoning, Slocum was being entirely unreasonable.

The trial was coming up right away, though, and Bartlet had high hopes, believing that Hyde would be convicted and would hang, and that the judge or the jury would dismiss the charges Slocum had on his men. But Oates was going to pull something. That was for sure. Bartlet figured that he would have to take his entire crew into town in the morning for the trial. Oates would. He was sure of that, and he did not mean to be caught outnumbered. He did not mean to allow Oates to steal Hyde away from the clutches of justice. Hyde would hang. Or if for some reason he failed to hang, he would for sure be gunned down. He would pay for his crime one way or the other. Bartlet swore to that.

Slocum had not expected any more trouble after the fiasco at the jailhouse on Saturday night, so he had left Tommy with his shotgun in charge of the five prisoners and headed back toward his hotel room. He was about to open the front door of the hotel when he heard his name called by a female voice. He turned and saw Terri Sue coming up the sidewalk behind him.

"Terri Sue," he said, "what are you doing out alone this time of night?"

"I heard the shots," she said. "Is everything all right?"

"It is now," he told her. "It's all over with."

"But what happened?"

He gave her a quick rundown of the evening's events. "Nothing to worry about," he said.

"Well," she said, "my sleep's been disturbed. I don't think I can go back to sleep again tonight. Could you stand some company?"

"You mean female company?" Slocum said.

"That was my meaning," she said. "More specifically, me."

"Sure thing, Terri Sue," Slocum said, offering her his arm. He opened the hotel door and walked her inside, across the lobby, and up the stairs to his room. Unlocking the door, he let her go in first, then stepped in behind her and shut and locked the door. He tossed the key onto a table, put his hat on a peg, and unbuckled his gunbelt and hung it on a bedpost. Not a bit shy, Terri Sue was stripping off her clothes. Slocum was not far behind her.

In another minute she was lying in the center of the bed with her legs spread wide apart, a delicious invitation. Slocum did not have to be invited twice. Her lovely white and smooth thighs were irresistible, with the marvelous mound cradled between them. The hair looked damp. Slocum crawled quickly on top of her. He kissed her lips, long and passionately. She responded by thrusting her tongue deep into his mouth, wandering around, exploring his teeth and tongue and the roof of his mouth.

Slocum's tool grew rigid and throbbed against her damp mound. She reached down for it and guided it into her happy wet hole. "Ah," said Slocum, as he eased into her, going deeper and deeper.

"Oh," she said. "Oh, yes."

Slocum pulled almost out, leaving only the head of his rod in her. Then he drove back in. Terri Sue thrust upward with her pelvis, taking the entire length. Then they both began to drive hard and fast, humping and thrusting like wild horses in the throes of mad and unbridled passion. They pounded against each other time and again, over and over, until at last Slocum exploded inside, sending surges of sweet liquid into her depths. Then lying side by side, they both went into a deep sleep.

Across the street, Tommy Howard had seen the two walk together into the hotel. He had waited and watched, but he had not seen Terri Sue come out again. He stood at the front window of the marshal's office, burning up inside with a terrible jealousy, a jealousy that was slowly turning into hatred for Slocum. He had taken this job with Slocum, thinking he would be helping out a notorious gunfighter. But so far, he had done all the shooting and all the killing and all the arresting. At least until Slocum had arrested the four riders from the Bartlet Ranch, an arrest that should never have been made, in Tommy's opinion. It seemed, at last, that Tommy had done all the work and Slocum was getting all the credit. Tommy Howard did not like that.

He was still standing at the window when Terri Sue came out of the hotel and headed for her home. In another minute or so, Slocum came out. He headed straight for the marshal's office. Tommy hurried back behind the big desk and sat down, placing his shotgun on top of the desk. When Slocum came in, everything appeared to be normal.

"No more problems?" Slocum said.

"No more," said Tommy.

"It's Sunday," Slocum said.

"I know that," Tommy answered, surprised at the edge on his own voice.

"Yeah," Slocum said. "Trial's tomorrow morning."

"And Oates and his boys'll be coming into town after Sammy," Tommy said.

"You're damn right they will," said Sammy Hyde from his cell.

"You keep your mouth shut," Slocum said to Sammy. He turned back to Tommy. "We need to be on alert from now on," he said. "There's no way to know when he'll strike. It could be now, or it could be after the trial."

"I've been on alert all the time," Tommy said.

"Yeah," said Slocum. "I guess you have been. Stay alert, but don't be too fast with that shotgun."

"You want me to wait for your permission before I shoot?"

For the first time, Slocum noticed the tone of Tommy's voice. He detected the resentment in it. He wondered what it was that was eating at Tommy. Finally he decided it was just the situation they were in. Tommy was not used to this kind of pressure. He decided to let it go.

"No," he said. "Use your judgment. I'm sure that you'll be fine. Why don't you take off and get some breakfast. Then get some sleep. I'll watch things here."

Tommy got up and walked out of the office, carrying

his shotgun. Slocum glanced out the window and saw that he was headed for the eatery. Then he went to the coffeepot on the stove and poured himself a cup. He took a sip and wrinkled his face. It was not nearly as good as the coffee that Terri Sue made at the eatery. It was coffee, though, and it would do. He sat down in a chair away from the desk.

"Hey, Marshal," said one of the four Bartlet men in jail, "when you going to let us out of here?"

"You're going to have a trial tomorrow morning," Slocum said.

"You got to be kidding," said the cowhand. "We done a public service."

"That's your view of the situation."

Another of the four cowhands stepped up to the cell door.

"We were on your side," he said, "but don't expect it again. When Oates and his boys come riding into town and acting like Quantrill and his men at Lawrence, don't expect no help from Bartlet."

"I don't need Bartlet," Slocum said. "Why don't you boys just shut up?"

"You better shut up," said Hyde, in the next cell. "If you don't, he'll throw a bucket of water on you."

"Slocum," said the first cowhand, "I'm going to ask you one more time. Are you going to drop those charges against us and let us out of here?"

"You've already heard my last word on that subject. I got no more to say."

"Shit," said the Bartlet man.

Over in the eatery, Tommy Howard was seated at a table, drinking coffee and waiting for his breakfast order.

Terri Sue had served the coffee and taken the order. Tommy, his shotgun laying across the tabletop, sipped at the coffee and stared at Terri Sue. He had to have her. Who the hell did Slocum think he was anyway? The King of Shot Creek? He'd only been in town a short time. He was lording it over everyone, including Tommy. He had his room paid for as well as all his meals and drinks. And he had a good paycheck coming to him. On top of all that, he was getting Terri Sue. Just then she came toward Tommy, carrying a coffeepot.

"You need a refill?" she asked.

Her voice was sweet and lovely, but to Tommy it was also deceiving. She was not sweet. She was sleeping with the town marshal. He had seen her go to his room with him and stay the rest of the night. She was a slut.

"Yeah," he said. "Thanks."

She poured his cup full and then said, "Your breakfast will be ready real soon now."

"Thanks."

Terri Sue walked away, and he watched her hips sway as she went. He tried to picture them undressed. He tried to picture Terri Sue totally undraped, tried to see her naked, tried to picture her breasts and nipples, her small waist. He tried to imagine himself on top of her, between her legs. He tried to feel what he would feel if his rod were sliding into her twat. She came back with his breakfast and put it on the table in front of him. He watched her hands.

"Anything else right now?" she said.

"No. I-I guess not."

"Just holler if you want anything, Tommy," she said.

He thought about her hands. They were lovely hands,

but he knew where they had been. Just last night and this morning, they had been fondling Slocum's cock. He knew that. He could see them in his mind's eye, wrapped around the engorged tool. Goddamn her. Goddamn Slocum.

16

Tommy finished his breakfast, but he drank more coffee. He did not want to take himself away from the company of Terri Sue, even though in his mind he kept cursing her. He cursed Slocum worse, though. Slocum had turned her the way she was. Goddamn Slocum. Tommy tried to consider his options. He could stay with Slocum and see this job through. That was what he had signed on to do. If Slocum did what he claimed he would do, he would ride away when the job was finished. Maybe Tommy would get the job. Town Marshal Tom Howard. It sounded good.

But then, maybe they wouldn't give him the job. What then? What would he do? He wondered if it would be worth his while to hang with Slocum. Take a chance on getting himself killed only to wind up with no job? That didn't make any sense at all. He had to think up something better than that. What were his options if he should leave Slocum to fight his own fight? There were two other sides: Bartlet and Oates. Both of them had lost men—might be needing more.

He could quit Slocum and hire on with one of the

135

two big ranchers. But which one? He thought about them. Oates might hold it against him that he had held a shotgun on him and his men that first day they rode in. He had gotten along better with Bartlet. He'd had two Bartlet men in the jailhouse with him for a few days. Bartlet might be his better choice. Bartlet.

But then, he wasn't so sure he should quit Slocum, not just yet. He did have some advantages as a deputy marshal. He was carrying that shotgun from the marshal's office, and it sure did make a difference when he faced gunhands. And he had been bossing cowboys around some. If he were to hire on as an ordinary cowboy, someone would be bossing him around. The way things were now, Slocum was the only boss he had. He liked that. He would like it even better if he were the boss.

He decided that he would stick with Slocum, but he would secretly be looking out for himself. But he wasn't sure how to do that. Start playing up to Church and Fall and any other councilmen he could locate to ensure that he would be named marshal when Slocum left? He wasn't much meant for ass-kissing. The idea did not appeal to him. His thoughts were interrupted when Terri Sue came back to his table again with the coffeepot.

"More coffee, Tommy?" she asked.

"Huh? Oh, yeah. Thank you, Terri Sue."

She poured his cup full once again, smiled at him, and walked away. Her smile hurt him. It was so pleasant, so sweet, but it hid the real Terri Sue, the slut who was sleeping with Slocum. The— No. He did not like calling her names. It was Slocum. He was the bastard. He was the one who needed cursing. He picked up his cup and took a tentative sip of the hot black liquid. It burnt his tongue. He put the cup back down and resumed his previous line of thought.

He had decided to stick with Slocum but to look out for his own interests, and he was trying to figure out just how to do that. He had already determined that his best bet, if he were to line himself up with one of the warring factions, would be Bartlet. He decided that while he had a little time left, he would ride out and see Bartlet. That's what he would do.

He got up from the table, leaving the hot coffee, and he paid for his meal on the way out. Hurrying to the stable, he got his horse saddled up, mounted, and headed for the Bartlet ranch. All the way out to the ranch, he tried to think about what he would say to Bartlet. When he finally arrived, he still wasn't sure what words he would use. He rode right up to Bartlet's front porch and dismounted. Bartlet had heard the approaching horse, and he came out on the porch.

"Well, hello, Tommy," he said. "What brings you out here? Has anything happened?"

"Oh, no, sir," said Tommy. "At least not yet."

There were chairs on the porch, and Bartlet invited Tommy up to take a seat. Tommy mounted the steps to the porch and sat down. Bartlet sat where he could face Tommy.

"Mr. Bartlet," said Tommy, "I came out to talk to you."

"All right," said Bartlet. "What about?"

"Well it's about that Sam Hyde, of course, and about Oates."

"What about them? There's to be a trial in the morning, isn't there?"

"Oh, yeah. That's still on. That is, it's still on unless Oates and his boys do something to stop it."

"They tried that once before," said Bartlet, "and as I recall, you stopped them."

"Yeah. That's right." Tommy smiled broadly. "With my shotgun."

"You think they'll try again after that?"

"I'm afraid they might. Of course, they'll do it different this time. They won't just ride up in front, open like, the way they did before. But they'll try something. I'm about sure of it."

"What makes you so sure?"

"I can't tell you that, sir, but I'm sure. Well, I'm pretty sure."

"What are you going to do about it?"

"I can't do nothing. Slocum won't believe me. That's why I came out to see you."

"Well, I'm glad you did. Do you have some plan? What should we do?"

"I don't rightly know, Mr. Bartlet. What seems to make sense don't seem to be right. At least, it sure ain't legal."

"What are you talking about?"

"Slocum leaves me to guard the jailhouse at night. If you and some of your boys was to come around tonight to get Hyde out of jail, I reckon I could be looking the other way."

Bartlet stood up and walked to the far end of the porch. He stood for a moment, turned, and walked back. He looked at Tommy.

"If we were to do that, what would we do with Hyde after we broke him out? Hang him? Shoot him? Deliver him to the courtroom in the morning?"

"I don't know about that. If you, or someone, was to break Sammy out of jail, I wouldn't know nothing about it after that."

"Hmm." Bartlet muttered and rubbed his chin.

"I know what'll happen though if Oates gets him out. He'll go free."

"Yeah. Yeah. That's right."

"I better be getting back to town now," Tommy said. "Maybe I'll see you later tonight."

Tommy stepped down off the porch and mounted his horse. He turned to ride out to the road, but he looked over his shoulder and saw Bartlet go back into the house. He paused. Then he looked toward the corral and saw a couple of Bartlet hands messing around there. He turned his horse and rode to the corral.

"Howdy, boys," he said.

"Howdy, Tommy," said one of the hands. "What are you doing out here?"

"Aw, I came out to see your boss. Told him that I think Oates is planning to make a move tonight. I think Mr. Bartlet means to beat him to the punch. Only thing is, I think he means to hold Hyde till time for the trial and then take him in to the courtroom. You know, even if he's found guilty, Oates won't let him hang. He'll bust him out first. But I don't think he'll be found guilty. I think Oates has paid off Church."

"Church? The mayor?"

"Yeah. He's going to be acting judge. See you, boys."

Tommy turned his horse and rode away, leaving the two cowhands scratching their heads. They watched Tommy until he was well out of earshot.

"What do you think, Red?" said one.

"Well, Melvin," said Red, "I don't think the boss will go too far with this."

"You think maybe we had ought to do it for him?"

"You know, I reckon maybe we ought to do just that."

Tommy rode back to town and went straight to the jail. Leaving his horse tied in front, he went inside. Slocum was sitting in a chair beside the desk.

"You get fed and rested up?" he said.

"Sure did," said Tommy.

"Then I'll do the same thing," said Slocum, standing up and heading for the front door.

"Take your time, Marshal," said Tommy. "I'll be okay here."

Slocum went outside and shut the door behind him. Tommy moved around the big desk and took his favorite seat. He placed the cherished shotgun on the desk.

"Hey, Tommy," said Sam Hyde. "How about some coffee?"

"All right," Tommy said, getting up again. "How about you boys?" he said to the Bartlet hands in the next-door cell.

"Sure," they said.

"Why not?"

Tommy poured them each a cup of his swill and delivered it into their hands. Hyde took a swig, made a face, and said, "Ugh."

Tommy said, "Hey, that's the best coffee you'll ever have again."

"Wiseguy," said Hyde. He took another sip and wrinkled his face. "Tastes like shit," he said.

Over at the eatery, Slocum was having a good cup of coffee, prepared by Terri Sue. She had no other customers for the moment, so she sat with him at the table.

"I guess you'll be leaving after the trial tomorrow," she said.

"No," he said. "If they find Hyde guilty, which I'm

sure they will, I'll have to stick around till the hanging's done."

"How long will that be?" she said.

"I don't know, but it'll be pretty quick."

"Well," she said, "we'll have to try to take advantage of what time we have left."

"Right now?" he said.

"I wouldn't mind," she said, "except I have to keep this place open yet."

"I guess I'll just have to be patient," Slocum said.

"Can you stand it?"

"I think so."

"Slocum?" she said.

"Yeah."

"Are you expecting any trouble before morning?"

"That's hard to say," he said. "Oates might try something. Then again, he might wait till after the trial. The only thing for sure is that Oates ain't going to let us hang Sammy Hyde without some kind of a fight."

"I hope you'll be careful. I'd hate for anything to happen to you."

"Don't worry," Slocum said. "As long as Tommy's got that shotgun, I'll be all right."

"He carried it in here with him to breakfast this morning," she said. "Laid it on the table in front of him like he was expecting some kind of trouble."

"He's in love with that shotgun," Slocum said. "I just hope it don't turn on him."

"Oh, he'll be all right. Won't he?"

Back in the jail, Tommy looked at the Bartlet cowhands in the cell. He looked at Sammy Hyde. He thought about what he had said to Bartlet and to the two

Bartlet hands. In a few hours, he imagined, someone would arrive at the jail with the intention of breaking all of the prisoners out. They would probably turn their companions loose first. Then all of the Bartlet cowboys together would unlock Hyde's cell. Probably Sammy would cower in a corner and beg Tommy to protect him. But the others would drag him out of the cell anyhow, because Tommy would simply go out the back door.

He would go out the back door and—but wait a minute. What would he tell Slocum? He couldn't just go out the back door, could he? He was supposed to watch Hyde carefully all night long. Maybe he could say he had to take a piss. Yeah. That would be it. Even Slocum couldn't hold that against him. Okay. So he would say that he had to take a piss and went out just for a couple of minutes. When he came back in, the cells were empty. He could say that he had no idea who did it.

It could have been Bartlet, in which case they would probably find Hyde's body hanging from a tree branch somewhere. On the other hand, it could have been Oates, he could say. Oates would have turned Hyde loose and maybe killed the Bartlet riders after taking them out of town.

He would tell Slocum that they could have a talk with both Oates and Bartlet, but that it probably wouldn't do any good. Likely they would just have to wait around and see if any body or bodies turned up. If it was Hyde's, then the guilty ones would be Bartlet hands. If it was the Bartlet cowboys, then it would be Oates's men. Tommy had it all figured out.

17

Bartlet thought very carefully over what Tommy had told him. It made sense. Still, Bartlet hesitated to ride into Shot Creek and take on the law. It just didn't set right with him. He stepped out onto his porch and looked around. The only cowhands he could see were Red and Melvin over at the corral. He yelled at them to come over. In another minute, they were at the porch. Bartlet invited them up to sit with him. He sat quiet, and Red and Melvin looked at one another, wondering what their boss wanted with them. At last he spoke.

"Boys," he said, "we've got a problem."

"Well, tell us what to do to help, boss," said Red.

"We'll do it," said Melvin. "Whatever it is."

Bartlet told the two cowhands what Tommy had told him. Then he told them his feelings about riding into town. Red and Melvin looked at one another again.

"Mr. Bartlet," said Red, "we'll take care of—"

"I don't want to know anything about it," Bartlet said, interrupting. "We never even had this conversation."

"Uh, yeah, boss," said Red. "Well, we better get back to work, hadn't we, Melvin?"

"Yeah. Back to work."

Bartlet stood up and went back into the house without another word. The cowboys stood up and looked again at one another.

"When we going, Red?" Melvin asked.

Tommy was sitting in the jail behind the big desk worrying. He had already set the events into motion, but then, he asked himself, where was the advantage to him? He had been too hasty. His jealousy, near hatred, for Slocum had blinded him. Suppose Bartlet or his boys did come in and break everyone out of jail. That would certainly get things going, but who would come out ahead? It could be anyone: Bartlet, Oates, Tommy, or Slocum.

He thought about getting word to Oates that Bartlet had plans. That would just about set the war off. He thought hard, nearly hurting his head. Thinking was not one of his best things. He was still trying to figure out where his best advantage lay. Tommy wanted promotion. He wanted Slocum's job with Slocum's benefits. And the more he thought about it, the less he could see any advantage coming to him from the range war. The trick was how to make himself out to be a hero. He would have to figure that one out, and fast. Time was getting short.

Slocum sat by the window in his hotel room, where he had a good view of the jail across the street. He cleaned and oiled his Colt and reloaded it. Then he did the same to his Winchester. He knew that trouble was coming, and it was coming soon, and he meant to be ready for it. The day so far, though, was very calm. There were few people on the street. No one seemed to be doing any business. Slocum figured that the citizens of Shit Creek must have been aware of the coming brouhaha. They were staying well hidden for their own safety. Slocum thought that if he had any sense, he would be far away from Shit Creek, for his safety.

He holstered the Colt, picked up the Winchester, put on his hat, and left the room. He went downstairs, outside, and down the street to Church's office. He found the mayor inside.

"Hello, Slocum," Church said.

"Mayor," said Slocum. "You all ready for court in the morning?"

"I'm as ready as I'll be," said Church.

"You know there'll be problems," said Slocum. "Before or after, there'll be problems."

"Yeah. I know that."

"I've got Tommy in the jailhouse with his shotgun," Slocum said, "and I'm keeping pretty close and keeping an eye out."

"So you're ready?"

"I didn't say that. Likely we'll be outnumbered when it happens. Be outnumbered pretty bad."

"Who do you think it will be?" Church asked.

Slocum shook his head. "It could be either one of them," he said. "Oates wants to save Hyde. Bartlet wants to see him pay."

"Bartlet should be content to let the trial go on," Church said.

"He would be if he didn't think that Oates will try to bust Hyde out."

"Yeah."

"If I were you," Slocum said, "I'd stay off the street."

"I will. Thanks for the warning."

Slocum walked out and headed for the eatery to see
Terri Sue. He wanted to give her the same advice he had
given Church. He did not want any stray shots catching
her.

Out on the Bartlet ranch, Red and Melvin rounded
up four other hands. They did not feel quite confident,
just the two of them, trying to pull off this job. They got
the boys together and sat around the bunkhouse. The rest
of the crew was all out chasing cows. Red rolled himself
a cigarette, while everyone else waited. He struck a
match and lit the smoke.

"Boys," he said, "me and Melvin are going into town
to get our pards out of jail." He stopped and looked over
the other four men. They sat silent. "It could be a pretty
big job for just the two of us."

One of the other four men spoke up. "You want we
should go in with you?" he said.

"That'd be good if you would," Red answered.

The cowhand looked at his three compadres. "That
sound all right to you fellows?" he said.

They all nodded and agreed. "Yeah," one said.

"Sure."

"You can count on us."

"That's good," said Red. "That'll make us six. When
we get the others out, we'll be ten."

"We get them boys out and get them their guns," said
one of the four, "we'll be pretty strong if we should
have to shoot our way out of town."

"That's right."

"Say," said another one. "What about that fucking
Sam Hyde?"

Red looked serious. He took a drag off his cigarette,

then looked up and into each of the faces of those seated around him.

"We'll get him, too," he said. "What do you think? Should we just shoot him in his cell, or should we take him out and hang him?"

"Red?" said one of the four.

"What is it, Frenchie?"

"We don't know what's going to happen when we get in there, do we?"

"How could we?"

"Well, I say let's just keep our minds open for whatever is happening. If it looks like we're going to have to shoot our way out of town, let's just shoot the bastard. If things goes smooth for us, let's bring him out and string him up."

"Sounds good, Frenchie. But I do got one more thing to tell you all. Tommy Howard's with us. He said he'd be looking the other way."

"Then all we got to worry about is that Slocum," Frenchie said.

That Slocum was at that minute sitting in the eatery with Terri Sue. Each had a cup of coffee. He had already warned her to keep off the streets for a while as much as possible. He told her that time was getting short, that the trial was at ten o'clock in the morning, unless someone did something to stop it before then. He and Tommy were going to do everything they could to see that the trial went on as scheduled, but there were no guarantees, of course. Anything could happen.

"Slocum," she said, "you don't owe anyone in this town anything. Why don't you just ride out? Get out while the getting's good. There are only two of you, and there are two whole cattle crews out there who will be coming in, each trying to get its own way. You won't stand a chance."

"It does look that way," Slocum said.

"Then you'll leave?"

"No."

"Why not?"

"It may be stupid," Slocum said, "but I don't run."

"Why not?" she said. "You said all along that you wouldn't stay here."

"I won't," said Slocum, "but I'll leave when the trouble's over. Not before."

Terri Sue looked at the table for a moment. She picked up her cup, but before sipping any coffee, she said, "In that case, you might stay here forever—in Boot Hill."

"Don't count me out yet," said Slocum.

He made some excuse and left. He was walking toward the jailhouse when he saw the children playing in the street. He hurried over to them and shouted.

"Get off the street, you kids. Hurry up. Go on. Go home and stay there."

The children scattered, and Slocum walked on. Visions of the boy who was killed swam in his head. He did not want to see anything like that happen again.

"Damn kids," he muttered as he walked on. He was trying to get the visions out of his head. They were the reasons he was still in this damned Shit Creek. The visions. He had seen plenty of men killed. Some deserved what they got and some did not. But the kid—he did not deserve it. He was just a kid. He hadn't done anything to anybody.

He began to get pissed off at both big ranches. Suddenly he wished that they would go on and start their damned range war and wipe each other out. Start it, but start it out of town, out where there were no kids to get in the way of their bullets.

Then it came to him. That was the thing to do. Get the war started but get it started out on the range. He tried to think how he would go about it. The nearest of the two ranches was the Bartlet place. He would go out there and agitate, start something, get Bartlet all riled up and ready to go to war. He hurried to the livery stable and saddled his Appaloosa. He rode past the jailhouse and shouted at Tommy. Tommy opened the door and looked out into the street.

"Hold things down, Tommy," Slocum said. "I'll be out of town for a spell."

He rode as fast as he could go to the Bartlet ranch and jumped off his horse and ran into the house without any invitation. Bartlet, seated behind his big desk working on his books, jumped to his feet and reached for a six-gun. Then he realized who had burst in on him. He put the gun down on the desk.

"Bartlet," said Slocum.

"What's the meaning of this?" said Bartlet.

"I came to warn you," said Slocum. "Oates and his men are planning to attack you."

"What?"

"The range war is on. He could be here any time now. You got to get your men together and get ready for him."

"Are you sure about this?"

"Of course I'm sure. Call your men together and get ready."

Bartlet picked up the gun again. He ran to the front

porch and began yelling for cowboys. Soon they were gathering around him. Slocum went back to his horse. Bartlet saw him and stopped him with a yell.

"Slocum," he said, "you ain't sticking around?"

"I'm the town marshal," Slocum said. "I shouldn't even have come out here to warn you, but I couldn't let Oates pull a sneak attack on you like that."

He turned his horse and hurried away. Reaching the road, he headed for the Simple Simon Ranch. He reached its main gate in half an hour. A couple more minutes found him at Oates's porch. Oates was sitting out in a chair, puffing a cigar, with a scowl on his face. Slocum dismounted and climbed the stairs to the porch.

"What the hell do you want here, Slocum?" said Oates. "You got no jurisdiction out here."

"I know that, Mr. Oates," Slocum said. "I ain't here on official business. In fact, if the town council ever finds out about this, I could be fired."

"What then?" said Oates. "What is it?"

"I just got word that Bartlet is getting his whole crew together and planning an attack on your ranch."

"What? Hell, I don't believe that."

"Believe it or not," said Slocum. "It's nothing to me. But if you ain't ready for him, he'll blow you off of this porch without giving it another thought. And then him and his men will burn the place to the ground."

"How'd you find out about this?" Oates demanded.

"I overheard a couple of Bartlet's cowhands talking about it in the Fat Back saloon. They were a little bit drunk and never even noticed me. Anyhow, I know it's out of my jurisdiction, but I can't stand to see anyone pull a dirty trick like that. I thought you deserved a warning at the least."

Oates's face took on a concerned look. He stood up, looked over his shoulder, and called out for some hands. Then he looked back at Slocum.

"Thanks," he said. "For a time I thought you were siding with Bartlet."

"I was just siding with the law," said Slocum.

"Yeah. I can see that now. Thanks for the warning."

"I got to get back to town now," Slocum said. "I shouldn't even be out here."

"Don't worry, Slocum. We'll be ready for the son of a bitch when he gets here."

18

Councilman Mike Fall walked into the office of Mayor Church and found him pacing the floor. Church stopped and turned to face Fall. He noticed that Fall was wearing a six-gun and carrying a Henry rifle in his right hand.

"Mike," he said, "what the hell are you up to? Slocum said we should stay off the street."

"Yeah, Will," Fall said. "You told me that already, but it doesn't seem right to leave two men to face all that trouble alone. You going to join me?"

"I don't know, Mike," Church said. "This is what we hired Slocum for, isn't it?"

"I guess so, Will. We hired Slocum and then Tommy to do our fighting for us. It seemed like the thing to do at the time. I agreed with you, remember?"

"Yes, you did."

"I didn't know it was going to come to this. I couldn't live with myself, Will. Not if I let this happen—just let it happen. I've got to help. Got to help some way."

"What are you going to do?"

"Go over to the jail, I guess. I don't know what else to do."

Church opened a desk drawer and pulled out a six-gun, which he began strapping around his waist.

"I may have a better idea," he said. "Tommy's at the jail with his shotgun. He can probably handle any trouble that might come there. Slocum will likely be with him."

"So?"

"So the real danger is if one or both of those big ranchers heads into town. We could ride out a few miles and hide on the side of the road—just in case. We could stop anyone who comes along that looks like they might be trouble."

"All right," Fall said. "You ready?"

"Let's go," said Church.

On the way out of the office, Church picked up a Winchester that stood in a corner of the room. They made their way quickly down to the livery stable, and along the way they picked up three other men willing to take a chance to defend their town. The five men moved out on the road that led to both big ranches.

Red and Melvin were riding into town alone. They had made their way off the ranch before Bartlet had called everyone together. As they moved along the road, they heard the sound of horses coming toward them. Red slowed his horse and made a gesture to Melvin, who followed him off the road into a thicket. They sat still while Church and the other four men rode past them. Then they moved out again.

Slocum was making his way back toward town on the same road at the same time. He was thinking about the big fight that should be taking place behind him at just about any time. It was the first time in his life he had deliberately provoked a big fight, a fight that would take a good many lives. He thought about that as he rode along, but he also thought about the kids who lived and played in Shit Creek, the kids whose lives would be jeopardized if he let the fight move into town. He had no regrets. He had just rounded a curve in the road when he heard someone call out.

"Stop right there," the voice said.

He halted the big Appaloosa and raised his hands.

"What is this?" he said.

"Oh, it's you, Marshal," said Will Church, stepping out of his hiding place to reveal himself to Slocum. Slocum lowered his hands.

"What's going on here, Church?" he said.

"There are five of us here," said Church. "We intend to make sure that no gang of riders gets into town— Bartlet or Oates or anyone else."

"That's a good idea, Mayor," Slocum said. "Hold the line. I think I'd better get back to the jail, though."

"We'll turn back anyone who tries to pass by here, Slocum," Fall said. "Don't worry about it."

Slocum rode on, but he rode easily. He was in no hurry, knowing that the road was guarded. If the Bartlet and Oates crews did not fail to engage one another on the road, and one of them tried to get through to town, the Mayor and his bunch would stop them. He had no reason to hurry—no reason that he knew of, anyway.

In town Tommy was nervous. He was up and pacing the floor. Every now and then he would go to the front window and look out. Then he would pace some more. The four Bartlet cowhands and Sammy Hyde in the other cell took note of it. Finally Sammy could stand it no longer.

"Goddamn it, Tommy," he said, "can't you set down?"

"Shut up," Tommy said. "Mind your own business."

"What you so nervous about?" Sammy said. "You thinking about Mr. Oates and the boys coming in for me again? I'd be nervous, too. They're going to kill you, you know."

"Shut your fucking mouth, you shithead bastard," Tommy said. "If you don't shut your goddamn mouth, I'll shut it for you, and I mean permanent. You understand that?"

Tommy waved the shotgun toward Sammy, and that was apparently all that was needed to shut Sammy's yap. But it made the Bartlet hands nervous, too.

"Hey, Tommy," one of them said, "if you pull that damned trigger, some of that shot will scatter over here."

"It might," Tommy said, snarling. He paced back to the window to look out onto the street again, and then he saw Red and Melvin riding in. His heart pounded in anticipation, but the two cowboys rode straight to the Fancy Pants saloon, dismounted, tied their horses in front, and went inside. What the hell? Tommy thought. What are those two dumb bastards doing? They're supposed to be over here. They said they would be, and I told them that I'd look the other direction. Goddamn it. Then he saw Slocum riding in. He went back behind the big desk and sat down.

Out on the road, Bartlet and most of his crew were just about to round the curve when a shot rang out. Bartlet hauled back on his reins and so did his men. About then, a voice called, "Hold it right where you are."

"Who's that?" Bartlet said.

"It's Will Church. I've got more men with me. No

one's riding into town today. Town's closed off. Turn around and head back to your ranch."

"Listen, Mayor," said Bartlet, "I got word that Oates is going in with his whole crew and—"

"Well, he hasn't gone by here, and you're not going by, either," Church said.

Bartlet looked around. He could not see Church, nor could he see anyone else who was hidden along the road. "You out here all by yourself, Mayor?" Bartlet asked.

"No, he ain't," said another of the mayor's men, his voice coming from a different location from that of Church.

"Far from it," said Fall, from yet another spot.

"There's more of us," said yet another voice.

"Bartlet," said Church, "you aren't planning to fight your way through us, are you?"

"No," said Bartlet. "No. I wouldn't do that. Turn around, boys. Let's head back."

They all turned their horses, and Bartlet rode through the crowd to be once again riding at the head. Then he led the men back the way they had come. They had gone about three miles when they saw the Oates crew heading straight for them. The Oates riders saw the Bartlets at about the same time. Both crews stopped and sat in the road, staring ahead at each other. Bartlet quickly calculated that he was outnumbered, but not by enough to make him back down.

"You're blocking my way, Bartlet," said Oates.

"Oh yeah? Just where the hell do you think you're going with that bunch?"

"We're on our way to town for a drink," Oates said. "Now, clear the road."

"Suppose you try to clear it," said Bartlet.

"You heard him, boys," said Oates. "Clear the god-damned road."

As he spoke, he raised his rifle and took aim. The Bartlet hands all started moving. Oates's shot missed any target. His cowhands had all their guns out, though, and were firing at anything they could see. Most of the Bartlet hands had jerked out their six-guns or rifles and were shooting back. In no time, just about everyone was hidden behind timber or brush. The shooting was sporadic.

Down the road, Church and his men heard the shots.

"Will," said Fall. "What do you think that's all about?"

"Sounds to me like Bartlet and his boys ran into Oates and his crew," said Church.

"What are we going to do?"

"Not a damn thing," said Church. "They're outside of our jurisdiction, you know."

He stepped out into the road with a grin on his face, looking in the direction of the shots. Gradually, the others stepped out with him. They all stared toward the shooting. Fall and Church looked at one another.

"Maybe they'll wind up the war right now," Fall said.

"Which side are you rooting for, Mike?" said Church.

"I'm kind of hoping they'll wipe each other out," Fall said.

Two of the other men were whispering to one another in the background. One of them stepped up to Mayor Church and said, "It don't look to me like you need us no more. I think we'll head back into town."

"Go ahead, Purdy," said Church. "And thanks."

"Sure thing, Mr. Mayor," said Purdy. Then he led the way back to their horses, leaving Church and Fall to guard the road. Purdy and the other two mounted up. They rode a short distance through the brush and stopped.

"Now what were you saying back there, Purdy?" asked one.

"I said that Oates and Bartlet's been causing our town all kinds of problems for a long time now," Purdy said. "Well, ain't they?"

"I don't reckon anyone could argue with that."

"Me neither."

"Did you hear what our councilman said back there?" Purdy added. "He's hoping that Bartlet and Oates will wipe each other out."

"Yeah. Not a bad idea."

"Well, I say, let's go help them."

"Oh, yeah. I get it."

"Let's go then."

They rode farther away from the road through the brush and thicket and then turned away from town. Then they traveled parallel to the road for some distance until they came to a small outcropping of hills. They rode up to the hilltop and moved along the ridge until they could see the battling ranchers down below.

"Get off your horses," Purdy ordered. "Hide them down on the hillside."

The three men dismounted and tied their horses down on the far side of the hill. Then they scampered back to the top and lay down with their rifles in their hands. Each man cranked a shell into the chamber of his weapon. One of the men looked at Purdy.

"Which side do we shoot at?" he asked.

"Shoot anyone who shows himself," Purdy said. "We don't give a damn which side we shoot."

Just then, a man showed himself from behind a tree.

He leaned out looking for a shot, and Purdy snapped off a round and dropped him.

"I think that was an Oates hand," he said. "I ain't sure."

The other two grinned, raised their rifles to their shoulders, and started looking for targets.

Down below, Bartlet was taking a bead on an Oates hand when the cowboy behind the tree next to him was stopped by a rifle shot. Down the road, Oates stood up from behind the huge rock where he was hidden and raised his rifle to his shoulder. There was another man just beside him. Oates fired and missed, and the other man stood up. Just as he did, a shot was fired and a bullet smashed into his chest. He fell back dead. Oates dropped quickly back behind the rock.

"You son of a bitch," he shouted at Bartlet.

"You dirty rotten bastard," Bartlet shouted back.

"Chickenshit."

"Scurvy shithead."

"Donkey dicks," shouted a third voice. All of a sudden, everyone on each side was screaming obscenities at everyone on the other side. Then someone fired a shot, and then everyone was shooting—everyone on both sides as well as the three men on top of the hill.

Back up the road, Church and Fall seemed to be enjoying the show. "It sounds to me," Fall said, "like they are just about to wipe each other out."

"For sure," said Church.

"You suppose we should ride up there and see what's happening?"

"After the gunshots have stopped, Mike. When everything has quieted down."

19

Tommy could stand it no longer. He picked up his shot-gun and stomped out of the office, leaving the prisoners alone in the jailhouse. He walked to the Fancy Pants saloon. He saw Red and Melvin standing at the bar. He did not want to be seen talking to them, but he felt like he had no choice. Looking around the room nervously, he walked to the bar, stood close to Red, and ordered a drink. With the drink on the bar in front of him, he lifted it and took a sip. Then he put it back down. Talking out of the side of his mouth, he said to Red, "What the hell are you two doing in here?"

"Just wetting our whistles, Tommy," was the answer.

"Why ain't you over to the jailhouse?"

"We're waiting till dark. We just come in a little early so we could have a drink or two. We'll be over there all right. Don't worry about us none."

"Right now is the best time," Tommy said. "Slocum's out of town somewhere. Far as I know, he might've left town for good with all this trouble coming up."

"He's out of town?" said Melvin. "Come on, Red. Let's go."

"Hold on," said Tommy. "We can't leave here together. Wait about five minutes after I leave."

"Okay," said Red. He picked up his glass.

Tommy downed his drink, turned, and left the bar.

Tommy walked out on the street, stood for a moment looking around, then headed back for the marshal's office. His heart was pounding in anticipation of the coming events. He had not yet decided what he was going to do. All he knew was that Red and Melvin were going to come into the jailhouse to get Sammy Hyde and to let their Bartlet companions out of jail. He gripped his shotgun tightly as he headed back.

Slocum was closer to town than were Church and Fall, but he, too, could hear the gunshots down the road. He knew what was happening. He had planned it, and it was working. The range war had started, and it had started outside of town, just as he wanted. He paused and looked back over his shoulder. Of course, he could not see anything. He rode on slowly, and he rode with mixed feelings. He had planned this battle. He had planned for a bunch of men to kill each other. He had never done that before. They weren't outlaws or particularly bad people. They were mostly a bunch of cowboys. But if he had not done what he had done, the fight would most likely have begun in town, and people who were even more innocent could have been hurt or killed. He rode on toward town.

Back down the road, behind Slocum, behind Church and Fall, the gunfight raged on. Oates glanced to his right just in time to see another of his men fall. This time, though, he could tell that the bullet came from above. He looked up toward the ridge and caught sight of a man with a rifle. He kept looking. Soon he had discerned that there were three men up there. He called out to one of his men hidden not far away from him.

"What is it, boss?" the man answered.

"They've got three men up on that ridge. We're easy targets for them."

The man looked up and saw some movement. "Yeah," he said. "I see where they are."

"Can you take a couple of men and go up there and get them?"

"Yes, sir."

In another couple of minutes, three Oates men were snaking their way through the brush and up the hillside. Gunshots continued around them. On the other side, Bartlet had a dead man on each side of him. He looked for a target. An Oates man peeked from behind a tree to shoot, and Bartlet picked him off. As he did, a rifle bullet smacked into the tree beside him, too close for comfort. He ducked to safety. He looked up at the tree. Then he looked toward the ridge.

"Goddamn it," he said. "Oates has got men up yonder."

"What was that?" said a cowhand.

Bartlet gestured toward the ridge. "He's got men up there shooting down at us," he said.

"I can go get them," said the cowhand.

"Take someone with you."

"You bet, boss."

Two Bartlet hands began working their way toward the ridge. A rifle shot from above knocked down another Oates man below. Now all rifles, Oates's men and Bartlet's, were pointed toward the ridge and firing. Purdy and the other two men ducked down low with bullets pinging around them.

"Goddamn," said one of them. "What do we do now?"

"Follow me," said Purdy. "We'll work our way down a little to the right."

He began creeping along the far side of the ridge, and the other two followed. Then an Oates man dropped over the ridge.

"Watch it," shouted Purdy.

One of his pards whirled, but the Oates man shot him first. Purdy fired, his bullet thudding into the Oates man's forehead. A second cowboy appeared on the ridge, and Purdy's remaining companion dropped him with a shot. A third cowboy came over the edge, and the man with Purdy stood up to shoot him dead. Just as he did, the first Bartlet hand, coming over the ridge, jerked out his six-gun and fired. The man with Purdy clutched his chest and toppled over the edge. Purdy made a sudden appearance just then. With his six-gun, he shot the Bartlet man, sending him sliding back down the hillside. The remaining Bartlet hand jerked off a quick shot that caught Purdy in the side. Purdy howled and twisted, and the man shot again, knocking Purdy down the far side of the ridge. Everything grew quiet. The Bartlet hand, the one man remaining up on the ridge, stood up and waved down toward Bartlet.

"I got them, Mr. Bartlet," he shouted.

From down below, Oates took careful aim with his rifle and squeezed the trigger. The man disappeared from sight. Everyone left alive commenced firing once more. This time, though, all the shots were from the road. The fight was fast and furious now. Oates and Bartlet had been after one another for some time, but now every cowboy there on both sides had lost good friends. Everyone was thoroughly pissed off. Everyone involved wanted everyone on the other side dead.

Tommy Howard settled back down behind the big desk in the office and waited nervously for Red and Melvin to make their appearance. They weren't moving fast enough for him. He wanted to get this over with and done. He had thought for a time that when Red and Melvin poked their noses into the jail, he would blast them with his shotgun and claim that he had stopped another jailbreak attempt. But there would be the four Bartlet hands already in jail. They would be witnesses, unless he killed them, too. And how would he explain that?

Red and Melvin downed the rest of their whiskey, looked at one another, and headed for the batwing doors. They were about to cross the street and head for the jail when they saw Slocum come riding in.

"Slocum," said Melvin.

"I see him," said Red. "Get out of sight."

They turned and went back inside to stand by the window and watch. Slocum pulled up in front of the jail, dismounted, and went inside.

"What now?" said Melvin.

"We keep out of sight of that son of a bitch," Red answered. "He can't stay up all night. When he goes to his room, we go to the jail."

Tommy jumped up when Slocum walked into the office. His eyes were wide. "Slocum!" he said.

"Who were you expecting?" said Slocum.

"Well, no one, I just-just didn't expect you so soon. That's all.

"Well, I'm back. Go on. Take yourself a break."

"I-I don't need—"

"Go on. Get yourself something to eat."

"Well, yeah. Okay. I will." He picked up the shotgun

and left the jailhouse. Slocum settled down in a chair against the wall.

"Slocum," called Hyde.

"What do you want?"

"Can I have some coffee?"

Slocum got up and walked to the coffeepot. He opened the lid and took a sniff.

"It don't smell none too good," he said, "but you can have some if you want it."

"I don't want to smell it," said Hyde. "I want to drink it."

Slocum poured a cup and carried it over to Hyde. He looked into the next cell. "What about you boys?" he asked.

"Unless you've got some whiskey," said one of them, "I'll pass."

"Suit yourself," said Slocum.

Tommy walked into the Fancy Pants saloon again. Red and Melvin were still standing by the window. He stopped not far from them. Red moved over close to Tommy.

"You said he wouldn't be there," he said.

"Well, I was wrong, wasn't I? How the hell was I to know he'd be coming back this soon?"

"Goddamn it. We believed you. We—"

"Oh, shut up, will you? Just wait till after dark like you planned in the first place. He'll go to his room after a while and leave everything to me. Then you can take care of it."

"All we got to do in the meantime," said Melvin, "is just keep our asses out of sight."

"Yeah," said Tommy. "That's right."

In his office, Slocum lit a cigar. He sent up a couple

of puffs, and then he looked over into the cells. He stood up and walked to the desk, opened a drawer, and pulled out a bottle of whiskey. Then he walked to the coffeepot, where there were several cups around. He poured six of the cups full of the whiskey. Then he carried five of them to the cells. He gave one to each of the prisoners.

"What is this, Slocum?" said one of the Bartlet boys.

"I got to thinking about it," Slocum said. "You all don't know it yet, but your bosses and their crews, all except you, are out on the road wiping each other out. The range war started without you. So let's all have a drink on it."

"Are you sure about that?" asked Hyde.

"There won't be anyone left to break you out of jail, Sammy," Slocum said.

"Why ain't you out there stopping it?" said one of the Bartlet boys.

"It's outside my jurisdiction," Slocum said. He took a drink of the whiskey. "Bottoms up, boys."

They all drank.

"How come they start fighting out yonder?" said Hyde.

"What?" said Slocum. "You want them to come into town and bust you out of jail?"

"Well, I—"

"Hell," said a Bartlet hand, "ain't no one coming in here to break you out. You're going to trial in the morning, and then you're going to hang."

The other Bartlets joined in laughing, and Sammy shouted at them, "You don't know that. Why, hell, I might be found innocent at the trial—if there's a trial. You don't know what the hell's going to happen. None of you do."

"You're going to hang all right," said another.

"I wish I had my gun," said Hyde. "I'd blast your asses all to hell."

"That's right," said a Bartlet hand. "That's your style, ain't it? We're in here without guns. That's the way you like to shoot people."

"Fuck you Bartlet bastards," said Hyde.

"Ain't no one getting a refill if you mean to carry on like this."

Sammy Hyde chugged down his share of the whiskey and held out his cup. "Hell, Slocum," he said. "We ain't carrying on about nothing. Are we, fellows?"

"No. Hell no," said the others.

Slocum laughed and poured drinks all around again. Then he sat back down.

Out on the road, Church and Fall still stood listening to the gunshots. They were fewer and further between now.

"The ranks must be thinned out somewhat by now," said Fall.

"I would imagine so," said Church.

"How much longer do we want to stay here?"

"I'd say till the shots quit altogether."

Down the road, Oates called his men around him. There were not nearly as many as there had been when the shooting started. They clustered around their boss, staying low behind boulders and trees.

"Men," Oates said, "this is getting to be boring. I say, let's stand up and meet them face-to-face in the middle of the road."

20

Church and Fall looked at one another. The shooting had stopped. It had been quiet for a few minutes now. "You think it's over?" Fall asked.

"Sounds like it," said Church. "Let's get our horses and take a little ride."

"Up ahead?" said Fall. "See what happened?"

"That's the general idea," said Church.

They walked to where their horses were tethered, got them loose, and mounted up.

"Come on," said Church.

They kicked their horses into a trot and headed up the road. It was still quiet. They moved faster. Coming on a curve, suddenly a shot was fired, then more. They stopped, dismounted, and ran for cover. Fall looked at Church.

"It's not over," he said.

"Obviously," said Church.

Around the curve, what was left of the two ranch crews was out in the middle of the road facing one another. Everyone on both sides was blasting away. Two of Bartlet's men went down, then one of Oates's. Bartlet took careful aim at Oates with his rifle and pulled the trigger, but the hammer just clicked. The rifle was empty. He tossed it aside angrily and pulled out his revolver. He snapped off two quick shots. One of them hit Oates in the left shoulder.

Oates cursed and raised his own rifle to his shoulder. Bartlet fired again, hitting Oates in the right thigh. Oates dropped to his knee. He raised the rifle again. This time he managed to get off a shot that tore through Bartlet's right biceps.

Back in the town, Slocum was beginning to feel a little buzz. He didn't mind. He figured the Oates and Bartlet boys were wiping each other out outside of town, if they hadn't already done so. He had no more worries. There would be a trial in the morning, and Hyde would be sentenced to hang. The Bartlet boys would likely get a slap on the wrist and be turned loose. It would all be over, and Slocum could get the hell out of Shit Creek. Besides all that, the bottle was empty, and the four prisoners were at least as drunk as he was. He stood up and headed for the door.

"Hey, Slocum," one of the Bartlet hands said, "where you going?"

"We're all out of booze, boys," he said. "I'm going to turn in."

"Hell," said another one. "It ain't dark yet."

"That's right," Slocum said, as he shut the door behind him, leaving the prisoners unattended. He walked out into the street, headed for his hotel room. At that same time, Terri Sue came out of the eatery. When she saw Slocum, she started walking toward him. They met in front of the hotel. Slocum tipped his hat.

"Howdy," he said. "You just lock up for the day?"

"Just now," she said. "Are you turning in so early?"

"Thought I would. Tommy's got everything under control, I guess." He realized as he said it that he did not know just exactly where Tommy was. He did not give a damn, though. He had already worked things out. He was not expecting any trouble.

"I don't suppose you'd want any company?" Terri Sue said.

"In my room?" he said.

"That was my meaning."

Just inside the Fancy Pants saloon, Melvin was standing at the front window. He saw Slocum leave the jail. He walked back to the bar, where Red was standing with Tommy, and he sidled up to Red.

"Slocum just left the jail," he said in a whisper.

Red glanced at Tommy standing on his other side. "The deputy's out, too," he said. "I guess the jail ain't guarded." He tossed down what remained of his drink and turned to walk out through the batwing doors. Melvin followed him. As they left, Tommy picked up his shotgun and fondled it. He waited a couple of minutes. Then he followed the two cowboys out the door.

Out on the road, two more cowhands bit the dust beside Bartlet. Bartlet got off another shot at Oates and hit him in the chest. Oates grabbed at his chest with both hands, dropping his weapon to the ground. He fell back, sitting down hard on his foot that was already underneath him from kneeling. His other leg was sticking out straight in front. His face wore a surprised expression. He had been totally shot, and Bartlet had done it. He had always believed that he would kill Bartlet. Now it appeared that things had turned out the other way around. He was astonished more than he was hurt.

Bartlet snapped off another round, which dropped Oates dead. At just about the same instant, three Oates hands fired into Bartlet. All of their bullets hit him, and he twitched and squirmed and twisted and at last fell over dead. There were two men left standing on the Bartlet side and three on the Oates side. They stood still, guns pointed at one another. They looked from one to the other. At last, one of the Oates men spoke.

"It's over," he said.

"Think so?" said a Bartlet man.

"Ain't no one left to pay us," said the first.

Church and Fall came riding up just then. When they saw what had happened, they stopped their horses. They sat in their saddles and looked down on the terrible scene before them. The five standing cowboys all holstered their guns. Church dismounted and walked to Bartlet's body. It didn't take much examination to tell that Bartlet was dead. Then he walked across the way to where Oates was lying. He found him dead as well. He stood up and looked around at all the cowboys.

"Well," he said. "I guess it's all over and done now."

"I reckon," said one of the hands.

"I guess you boys will all be moving on now," Church said. "Looking for jobs."

"What'll become of the ranches?" said a cowboy.

Church shrugged. "I don't know," he said. "The court'll have to figure it out."

"I'll be riding out," said a cowboy. He walked toward his horse. Slowly, one at a time, the others followed his lead. Soon Church and Fall were left standing alone on the road in the midst of all the bodies.

"We'll have to tell Gool to bring a wagon out here," Fall said.

"He'll want to know who'll pay," said Church.

Slocum and Terri Sue were in Slocum's room. She was lying on her back in the middle of his bed. He was between her legs, pumping for all he was worth. Terri Sue clasped her ankles together at the small of Slocum's back, and each time he thrust downward, she thrust up to meet him. Their bodies slapped together rhythmically. Whop. Whop. Whop. Terri Sue moaned with each slap. "Oh," she said. "Oh. Oh. Oh." Slocum pounded until he was almost worn out with the pounding. Then he stopped. He breathed deeply for a few seconds. Then he pulled out.

Terri Sue wondered what was wrong. Why had he stopped? Then he took hold of her waist with both hands and turned her over. She scrambled up onto her knees and reached back between her legs to find his still-rigid tool. Then she guided it back into her hole. "Ahh, yes," she said. Slocum began pounding again. The rhythmic slapping resumed.

Down below, Red and Melvin approached the jailhouse door. They stopped and looked at one another. Then Red opened the door and walked in with his six-gun drawn. There was no one in the office, only the five men in the two cells. Melvin followed Red inside and shut the door.

"Red. Melvin," said one of the Bartlet boys.

"Hey, get us out of here."

"Get the keys, Melvin," said Red.

Melvin ran to the desk and rummaged a minute or so

for the keys. He found them and ran to the cell to unlock the door. The four Bartlet boys were out in no time.

"Where are your guns?" said Red.

"In the desk," said one of them. Without waiting for anyone else to make a move, he went to the desk and found them. Pulling them out of the drawer one at a time, he passed them around to their owners. As the cowhands strapped on their guns, Red took the keys to the next cell and walked to the door.

"What are you doing?" said Sammy.

"I'm fixing to let you out of that cell, boy," said Red.

"No."

"You want your trial, do you?"

"No. I—yes."

Red unlocked the door.

"I guess the trial tomorrow will be pretty calm," Fall said to Church as they approached Shot Creek.

"I imagine that it will be," said Church. "With Oates out of the way, there won't be anyone to oppose it."

"There's only one way it can go," said Fall.

"We can't ever say that," Church said. "In this country, a man is innocent until he's proven guilty. He can have his witnesses and his defense lawyer. And he'll have a jury, too. We'll just have to wait and see what the jury's decision is."

"It will be 'guilty,' " Fall said.

The town was just ahead. In no time they would be riding past the livery stable. The sun was getting low in the sky, and the town seemed unusually quiet.

Upstairs in his hotel room, Slocum had just finished with his lustful work. Terri Sue was still lying in the middle of the mattress with a smile on her face. Slocum sat up on the edge of the bed. He found a cigar and lit it. He walked to the window and looked out. Tommy was still on the sidewalk close to the saloon. Slocum did not see him. What he saw was a very quiet street. It did not make sense to him. He began to get dressed.

"Slocum?" said Terri Sue.

"What?"

"Is anything wrong?"

"Not with you," he said.

"What is it?"

"I just ain't sleepy no more," he said. "I'm going out. You just stay here and take it easy. I'll see you later."

"I don't believe you," she said. "There's something else, isn't there?"

Slocum finished strapping on his gunbelt. He got his hat off the peg on the wall and set it on his head. He gave Terri Sue a last look. "It's just too damn quiet out there," he said. "I'm going to take a look."

Inside the jail, Red had unlocked the door to Sammy Hyde's cell. Hyde had pressed himself against the far wall, so Red and Melvin had gone inside. When they came close to him, Sammy kicked at them.

"I ain't going with you," he said. "I'm in jail. You can't do this."

He kicked out again, and Red grabbed his foot and pulled him down onto his back. Melvin took hold of the other foot to keep Sammy from kicking. The other cowhands crowded into the cell and secured Sammy's arms. Then they jerked him to his feet, but his knees grew weak and he collapsed. They heaved him to his feet again and held him up.

"Get him outside," Red said.

They started dragging him out of the cell. When they started to go through the door, Sammy suddenly found some more strength. He managed to grab hold of the bars and tried his best to keep the men from getting him through the door.

"Let me go," he screamed.

Outside, Tommy heard the scream. He had not planned it this way. Someone else might hear. He had to do something, and he had to do it quick. He cocked the shotgun and started to run toward the jail.

Slocum had heard it, too, and he started moving fast from the front door of the hotel. As he moved, he pulled out his Colt. The mayor and the councilman had just ridden in front of the livery stable. They heard the screams of Sammy Hyde and saw the two lawmen running toward the jail. They halted their horses and looked at one another.

"Who could it be?" said Fall.

"Let's just wait here," Church said. "We'll find out soon enough."

There were two more watching, unknown to the rest. In Slocum's room, Terri Sue stood at the window. She heard the shouts coming from the jail, and she saw Tommy run, and then Slocum. She wondered what was up. Slocum had been wrong about something, for he had thought that everything was all right. What could it be?

And just inside the Fat Back saloon, standing at the front window, Mo Diamond stood watching.

21

Tommy came to an abrupt halt when he saw the cowhands crowding their way out the front door with poor sniveling Hyde in their grasp. Hyde was using his hands and feet in a vain attempt to keep them from getting him through the door. Tommy stood for a moment, hesitant, trying to decide what the hell to do. He sensed that he had but an instant to make up his mind. The cowboys were taking the prisoner out of jail. He would be justified. He would even be hailed as a hero for preventing the jailbreak. He raised the shotgun and blasted them. Hyde, being in the middle of the crowd, took the brunt of the shot. His face and chest were a mess of blood, and he went limp in the arms of the cowboys.

"Tommy, you damn fool," Slocum shouted.

The two cowboys closest to Hyde were also hit by the blast. They, too, went limp and sagged to their knees, one falling forward onto the sidewalk. The remaining boys, including Melvin and Red, were a little peppered. They scrambled back into the jail, pulling out their six-guns. Red tried to shut the door, but the fallen men were blocking the way. The cowboy who had been on Hyde's left was hit bad, but he was still alive. Red grabbed him by the shirt and dragged him inside.

Melvin saw Slocum out in the street, and he fired a shot. Slocum ducked into the darkness of a doorway. Just at that moment, the three remaining Oates cowhands rode into town. Fall and Church heard them coming and turned in their saddles.

"What are you men doing here?" said Church.

"What's going on?" was the answer he got.

"We don't know," said Fall. "We just got here."

"That was a gunshot," said a cowhand.

"We could tell that," Fall said.

"Well, let's ride on in and see what's up."

"We're staying right here till it's over," said Church.

"Well, I'm going on in," said the cowhand. He looked at his two buddies. "What about you?"

"Let's go," said one of them.

The three cowhands kicked their horses and headed on into town toward the sound of the shot.

Red grabbed Melvin and pulled him back.

"You damn fool," he said.

"It's that Slocum," Melvin said. "He was coming this way."

"We might've tried talking to him," said Red.

"His goddamn deputy has already double-crossed us, ain't he?" Melvin said. "He was supposed to stay out of the way."

"He's out there now," Red said. "I ought to kill him right now."

"There's Slocum and Tommy out there," said Melvin. "We've got them outnumbered."

"Gabe ain't worth much right now," said Red.

The three Oates cowhands rode up just then and spotted Tommy, who had moved back to the sidewalk across the street from the jail. Slocum was a couple of doors down, still in the doorway.

"Get out of the street," he shouted.

One of the cowboys looked in the direction of the voice. "What's going on here?" he asked.

"Jailbreak," Tommy shouted. "Get out of the way."

"Who is it?"

"Bartlet's men," Tommy answered. "Get out of the street."

The cowboys rode to a hitch rail and dismounted. They stepped up on the sidewalk and stared across the street at the jail.

"You in the jail," Slocum called out. "Toss out your weapons."

"The hell," shouted Melvin.

"Shut up, Melvin," said Red. "Hey, Slocum."

"I'm listening."

"What's the deal?"

"No deal," Slocum said. "Just toss out your guns."

"Then what happens?"

"Then you go to jail," Slocum said, "and wait for your trial."

"They're goddamned anxious to have a fucking trial in this town," Melvin said.

"Shut up, Melvin," said Red. "Hey, Slocum. We got a hurt man in here."

"Toss out your guns, and we'll get him tended to."

"He might bleed to death."

"It's on your head. Toss them out."

"We ain't tossing out our guns, but I'm sending Gabe out. He needs help."

"Don't do it," Tommy shouted.

Red turned to Gabe. "Can you stand up and walk?" he asked.

"I think so."

"Leave your gun here. They won't shoot an unarmed and hurt man. Go on now."

Gabe stood unsteadily on his feet. Melvin pulled the gun out of Gabe's holster. Red helped hold him steady and pushed him toward the door. Gabe stepped in the doorway. He stood for a moment wobbling.

"Here he comes, Slocum. Don't shoot. He's wounded."

Tommy raised a six-gun and fired. The bullet hit Gabe in the sternum, splattering blood back on Red and Melvin. Gabe's body fell back into the doorway. Red caught it in his arms.

"Goddamn," he said. "They killed him dead."

"It was that damned deputy," said the third cowboy.

"What'll we do, Red?" said Melvin. "We're damn sure outnumbered now, and if they'll shoot a man like Gabe, they'll kill us for sure."

Red looked around. "Let's go out the back door," he said. "Maybe we can sneak around and pick up some horses."

"Maybe we can sneak up behind that damn deputy and blast his ass to hell," said Melvin.

"Maybe so," Red said.

He fired a shot out the front door, and then crouched low and ran to the back door. Melvin and the third cowboy followed him. The next few minutes were deathly quiet. Slocum stepped out on the sidewalk, Colt in hand. No shots came from the jail.

"Tommy," he said, "get over there and check things out."

"Me?" said Tommy.

"You, you little shit. Get on over there."

Tommy stepped cautiously into the street.

"Go on," said Slocum.

Tommy crossed the street with slow and tentative steps. It seemed to take him forever to get over to the other sidewalk. He then stepped quickly up on the boards and pressed himself against the wall away from the jailhouse door. Then he sidled down to the doorway. There were two bodies in his way, but he managed to step over them to get inside. The back door was standing open. No one was inside. Leaning over the corpses, he called out the front door. "They're gone," he said. "No one's here."

Slocum stepped out into the street, and then the three Oates cowboys followed him. They all walked across to the jail. Sammy Hyde was dead. So were two of the Bartlet cowhands. Outside, Church and Fall rode up. When they saw the five men on the street investigating the jailhouse, they dismounted and joined them.

"What happened here?" Church asked.

Slocum looked at Tommy and said, "You tell him. You caused it." Then aloud, he said, "Someone go fetch Gool and get this mess cleaned up."

"Well, Mayor," Tommy said, "I was just coming back to the jail when I seen a bunch of cowhands coming out with Sammy—"

"You left him unguarded?" said Church.

"Well, just for a minute. I—"

"There's two dead cowhands here," said Slocum, interrupting. "How many are left?"

"There was four in jail," Tommy said. "Two come in to break them out."

"Two dead. That leaves four. Tommy?"

"Yeah."

"Did you see the two come riding in? Did you see them go in the jail?"

"No. I, uh, I never seen them till they was coming out with Sammy. That's when I seen them."

"And that's when you shot," said Slocum.

"Yeah. Well, I had to think fast. I—"

"How do you know it was two men who come in to break them out?"

"Hell, I seen them. I—"

"Never mind," Slocum said. "We'll take it up later. Right now, we have four cowboys to locate."

"You want some help, Marshal?" asked one of the Oates hands.

"Not from you, pardner," Slocum said. "You three get your ass off the streets. I recommend the Fancy Pants saloon."

The cowboys looked at one another and then headed for the Fancy Pants. Slocum turned to Tommy. He gestured to his left.

"Get yourself down to that end of the block and check around the corner. Look back in the alley. Be careful."

Tommy reloaded his shotgun and headed for the end of the block. Slocum turned and went the other way.

In the alley, Melvin had gone to his left when he went out the back door. The other cowboy had gone right. Red had been moving along behind Melvin, but he came to a stairway that led up to the roof of one of the buildings. He went up there, thinking that he would get a good look around the town that way.

Down below, Tommy rounded the corner to the alley just as Melvin appeared. Both men were startled and shouted out. Tommy raised his shotgun and fired before

Melvin could pull his six-gun. The blast sent Melvin flying back through the air. He splattered on the hard ground. He was unrecognizable.

At the other end of the alley, one of the Bartlet cowboys heard the shotgun blast. It scared him back against the wall. Someone had scurried around to the alley. He had no idea how many. He did not think that there were any more than Slocum and his deputy, but he wasn't sure.

"Hey, cowboy," said Slocum. "Drop your gun and step out here."

The cowboy felt cold fear. He started trembling. "You'll kill me," he said.

"You drop your gun like I said, and I won't shoot you."

"We didn't think you'd shoot Gabe," said the cowboy. "We never thought your fucking deputy would shoot us, neither."

Things started coming together in Slocum's mind. He'd had his suspicions, but now he was just about sure. "I didn't think so, either," he said. "I won't shoot you. You have my word."

The cowboy unbuckled his belt and let it drop to the ground. Then he stepped out of the shadow.

"What's your name?" Slocum asked.

"They call me Slender," said the cowboy. "My name's Chester McGee."

"Well, Slender," said Slocum. "Tell me what you meant about Tommy—my deputy. What did you mean you didn't think he'd shoot you?"

"Red had a deal with him," Slender said. "He said they could come in and get that Sammy Hyde out and us boys as well, and he'd be looking the other way."

"He said that, did he?"

"That's what Red told us he'd said."

"Where's your horse, Slender?"

"I don't know. I was in jail."

"If I walk you to a horse, what would you do?"

"I'd mount up and ride the hell out of here—north."

"Pick up your gun, Slender, and let's go."

Slender hesitated an instant, then picked up the rig he had dropped. Slocum motioned him toward the street, and they walked together around to the front of the building. Slender gestured toward two horses tied in the street.

"Those're Bartlet horses," he said. "Must be the ones Red and Melvin rode into town."

"Come on," said Slocum. He walked Slender to the horses. Slender mounted up. "On your way, boy," Slocum said, and Slender turned the horse to ride away. Mayor Church came running up.

"What is this?" he said.

"No charges against this boy," Slocum said.

Slender turned the horse and started riding out of town. Up on top of a building across the street, Red looked over the edge of the false front. He was astonished to see Slocum allowing Slender to get away. He stood up to see better, and Tommy, having just returned to the street, happened to look up. He spotted Red. Tommy raised his shotgun and thumbed back the hammer. Mo Diamond stepped out the front door of the Fancy Pants saloon, pulling his Colt as he moved. He fired one shot into Tommy's back. Tommy fell forward in the street, dead.

Slocum ran over to the body and checked it. He stood up and faced Diamond.

"What the hell you do that for?" he asked.

Diamond pointed to the figure on the roof. Red was

standing there with his hands in the air. "Your deputy was about to blast that man there," he said.

Slocum looked up at Red. "Come on down here," he said.

When Red came down, he confirmed the story Slocum had been told about Tommy. In Slocum's mind there did not seem to be any more to do. He pointed at the other Bartlet horse. "If you head out now," he said, "you might be able to catch up with Slender."

Unbelieving, Red mounted up and lit out. Slocum explained things to Church. Then he took the badge off his chest and handed it to the mayor.

"Are you sure you won't stick around, Slocum?" asked Church. "Be an easy job now."

"Church," Slocum said, "I can't get far enough away from the stink of this place or fast enough away from this goddamn job."

It took him a few minutes to get his horse from the stable and his gear from his room. He had not been in Shit Creek for near a month, and he did not even bother collecting any salary from Church. As he rode south out of the town and away from the memory of the distasteful job, he hoped that no one outside of the wretched place would ever hear of the episode. He did not want his reputation to be stained beyond repair.

Watch for

SLOCUM AND THE WIDOW'S RANGE WARS

345th novel in the exciting SLOCUM series
from Jove

Coming in November!